All the Beggars Riding

LUCY CALDWELL

faber and faber

First published in this edition in 2013
by Faber and Faber Limited
Bloomsbury House,
74–77 Great Russell Street,
London WC1B 3DA

Typeset by Faber and Faber Ltd

Printed in the UK by CPI Group (UK) Ltd, Croydon CR0 4YY

Quotations from Louis MacNeice's 'London Rain', 'Autobiography' and 'Snow' are
taken from *Collected Poems* © Estate of Louis MacNeice and reprinted by
permission of David Higham Associates.

Quotations from Sylvia Plath's 'Metaphors' and 'Winter Trees' are taken from
Collected Poems © Estate of Sylvia Plath and reprinted by permission of
Faber and Faber Ltd.

The right of Lucy Caldwell to be identified as author
of this work has been asserted in accordance with Section 77
of the Copyright, Designs and Patents Act 1988

A CIP record for this book
is available from the British Library

ISBN 978-0-571-27055-2

FSC
www.fsc.org
MIX
Paper from
responsible sources
FSC® C101712

2 4 6 8 10 9 7 5 3

For Maureen and for Peter, for everything

The rain of London pimples
The ebony streets with white
And the neon-lamps of London
Stain the canals of night
And the park becomes a jungle
In the alchemy of night.

My wishes turn to violent
Horses black as coal –
The randy mares of fancy,
The stallions of the soul –
Eager to take the fences
That fence about my soul.

from Louis MacNeice,
'London Rain'

Late May, a Thursday, the morning. Early morning, say six, or half six, but the sunlight is already pouring in, through the curtainless window set high in the slope of the roof, over the narrow bed and the sheets and the bare boards of the floor, flooding the room and everything in it, so that everything feels lit from inside. You are standing, face upturned to the window, breathing in the sun. I can see you, almost: if I close my eyes I can almost see you. A Thursday morning in May, 1972.

You've waited for this day, counting down each morning, as you wait for every second Thursday. Sometimes the waiting – delicious, unbearable – is almost better than the day itself, when it finally comes. The waiting, now, is like a bubble in your chest, and you are light and breathless with it.

You'll walk into work today, take the long way and go through Regent's Park. The flower-beds, the rose garden: they'll all look like they're laid out for you, especially, and today.

The weather has been unsettled lately, cloudless mornings turning into gusty skies and spatters of rain by mid-afternoon. You're going to go to the cinema – you decided this on the phone last night – a special screening at the Odeon on High Street Kensington of *Doctor Zhivago*. You haven't seen the film, and neither has he. Afterwards you'll dander (his word, your new favourite) back to Earl's Court, buy groceries on the way, a bottle of red wine, and you'll cook something simple. Extraordinary how even the simplest of things – the buying of eggs and tomatoes and cheese, the slicing of a lettuce, the pouring of wine into a glass – is transfigured by love. Love. The bubble swells in your chest. You haven't said it yet, neither of you, but maybe tonight he'll say: I love you, Jane. I love you.

The slight shadow that attempts to lace over the edges of things – your mind, the day – you push away.

It's a Thursday morning, an early Thursday morning, in May 1972, and you are poised on the edge of it, of everything. You walk over to the record player, propped on a crate in the corner, and put on a record: the B-side of Van Morrison's 'Come Running/Crazy Love'. You play it so quietly it's barely audible – the house is still and the others asleep – but you know the words inside out by now, after two weeks of playing them over and over, until they seem woven into the very fabric of you. Silently, inside, you sing along, and start to take the foam curlers from your hair. You slept in them, so that the curl would take, and when you unpin your hair after work the wave should still be there.

You wouldn't change anything, you suddenly think. You don't know where it comes from, or if it's an illusion, a trick of the sunlight and the music and a sleepless night, but you know, just know, that everything, in the end, is going to be fine.

THE CHERNOBYL EFFECT

The Chernobyl Effect

The Chernobyl Effect was the name of the documentary. It was what started things. Late one mid-week channel-crawling night.

It was one year after my mother died, almost to the date, and I had suddenly realised that I was an orphan now. 'Orphan': it sounds ridiculous to call yourself an orphan at the age of almost forty. But that evening, out of nowhere, it hit me – I felt it in my chest, like something physical – I was truly alone in the world.

My mother was ill for a long time before she died. She suffered from heart disease, which is a grim sort of irony: intrinsic cardiomyopathies, to give the condition its medical name. Unpredictable weaknesses in the muscle of the heart that are not due to an identifiable external cause. It's one of the leading indications for heart transplant, and indeed she should have, could have, been on the register for one, except that at every stage she point-blank refused. It was her heart, she said, over and over. She didn't want it ripped out of her – she was occasionally, surprisingly prone to melodrama like that, my mother – and she didn't want someone else's heart in her. The drugs they gave her to try and stabilise her, as her condition deteriorated, caused her much suffering and weakness and confusion, but still she wouldn't change her mind. She was stubborn as hell, my mother, when she set her mind to something. She was young, too: only fifty-nine when she died. Sometimes it felt like one more thing she'd set her mind upon, although it wasn't as if she was religious, or believed in any grand reconciliation or redemption after death.

So, anyway, she'd died, and for the first few months things had been indescribably bad, even though we weren't particularly close. From the outside, I managed to look like a normal person: phoning the agency, getting my rota, seeing the patients, shopping, cooking, all the mundane rest of it. But inside I was alternately blank and lurching with grief, thick and oily, like waves, that would rise up and threaten to swamp me utterly. I won't try to describe it any more: I'll only sound histrionic. People kept saying, time will heal, and in a terrible, clichéd way, it does: every day life pastes its dull routines over the rawness, although the rawness is still there. Six months after, I'd begun to feel that I was surfacing; on a good day I might even be above the water, although of course without warning you can still be dragged back under. Then everything happened with Jeremy, and terrible as that was, it was galvanising in the sense that some kind of survival mechanism kicked in and there was so much practical stuff to sort out – a bit like the immediate aftermath of a death – that I was on autopilot for a while.

I'm not explaining this very well: I'm getting everything jumbled up together. Which, in a way, is what it was; but that doesn't help the telling of it. I suppose what I'm trying to say is that I thought I'd come through the worst of it, when that night – two weeks ago now – I came across that programme on the TV and everything changed.

The documentary was about the aftermath of those explosions that destroyed the fourth reactor at the nuclear power plant near Pripyat on the 26th of April 1986. I hadn't thought about it in years, but as soon as I saw those infamous, grainy satellite photos of the power plant matchsticked and smouldering, and the rubber trunk-nosed radiation suits, it all came back to me. Sitting cross-legged with Alfie on the brown shagpile rug through *Newsround* and then all of the other news bulletins we could find, right through to the *Nine O'Clock News* and BBC2's *Newsnight*, at which point our mother came home from work and made us switch off the television, saying it would give Alfie nightmares, which it did, of course: how could it not? The Soviet government was equivocating, and they were starting to detect radiation as far away – as near – as Glasgow. People on panel discussions were saying things like 'Is this the end of the world as we know it?'

Our world, that is, Alfie's and mine, and our mother's, had come to a sudden, messy and public end the autumn before. Sunday 24th November 1985: the date is seared in my memory. I was twelve, then, twelve and four months, and Alfie had just turned eight, when our father was killed – a freak accident, a helicopter crash in bad weather. Then came the revelations, and the reporters, and soon after that we had to move out of our home and into the grotty, ramshackle rooms on the North End Road. Unsurprisingly I had shut down: closed in on myself so tightly that nothing got through, or touched me, until I saw those first shaky BBC images.

Within a millisecond or so of flicking to the channel, in less than the time it took me to realise what it was, this swirling, churning welter of things was set going inside of me. As if all the griefs in my life, my father, my mother, and to an extent Jeremy, as if I was mourning all of them: mourning myself and all my other selves.

I'm getting ahead of myself, I know, jumbling things up again. I do intend to come to things properly, in their own time, in at least approximately the right order. It's harder to tell a story, though, than you'd think. As I said earlier, lives aren't orderly, and nor is memory: the mind doesn't work like that. We make it so, when we narrate things – setting them in straight lines and in context – whereas in reality things are all mixed up, and you feel several things, even things that contradict each other, or that happened at separate times, or that aren't on the surface even related, all at once. So I need somehow to convey the sensation of chancing on this documentary, so late at night, when what I was probably searching for and expecting was something banal and mind-numbing, anaesthetic, like reruns of *Friends*. Seeing the Chernobyl footage, and understanding on my pulses what it was, and the surreal sensation of being there a year after my mother died and at the same time it being five months after my father had died: as if both things, both times, were happening at once. I'm really not explaining this very well. It was as if there was no distinction between times and they were all just overlaid on top of each other, the same things happening again and again on their little loop in a hellish eternal present. And in that instant, I knew I had to do something: I was trapped and I needed to do something, change something, before it was too late.

If you've ever had a panic attack, you'll know what I mean. The feeling of everything happening at once, everything closing down on you, and in on you, and there being no way out, and worse than the physical is – and yes, this sounds over-the-top, too, but there's no other way of putting it – a creeping, almost existential, sense of doom.

The thing I just said, about separating strands out, and putting them in order, a beginning a middle and an end, and trying to understand them: that moment is when I decided – more than decided, *knew* – that that was what I needed to do, had to do. As if the telling of the story could somehow save me.

Perhaps things will make more sense once I have explained the documentary a little.

The Chernobyl Effect was made maybe ten years after the catastrophe. It consisted of a series of interviews with survivors from Pripyat and evacuees from the surrounding villages, and two doctors or scientists with deliberately distorted voices and blacked-out eyes. The doctors, or scientists, were the least interesting: they talked in solemn chains of statistics and made predictions about percentages and roentgens per hour. But the survivors – or 'victims' might be a better word, because there was nothing triumphant about them, no sense that they'd overcome – they were twitching and palsied, clinging on to life by their flaking fingernails. Hardly any of the men spoke. It was the women who wanted to tell their stories. The women, with their craggy, sunken faces and teeth like pickled walnuts, looked like grandmothers – older than grandmothers, like ancient crones or hags from Belarusian folk stories. But most of them were no older than me, and some of them were five, ten years younger. When the reactor exploded, they'd been nineteen, twenty-one, twenty-four. Newlyweds, young mothers, strong, healthy wives. Most of their menfolk worked at the plant, and they supplemented the wages by keeping chickens, and maybe a cow; by growing potatoes, cabbages, and a few rows of black radishes. The day of the explosions was a Friday. At about midday, word got around that there was a fire at the plant. As the sun set, they watched it in the distance, and it was wilder and more beautiful than you could ever imagine, they said, the flickering streams of colour and shining light, like something from an American movie. They piled outside to watch it, passed around bottles of the local spirit, let their children stay up way past their bedtime. The word had spread to villages further afield by this time, and family, friends came in cars or on bicycles to see the unearthly light and the showers of sparks – like fireworks, on an indescribable scale – holding their children on their shoulders so they too could see and remember. No one knew how dangerous it was. Even the next morning, when the streets filled with tanks and gas-masked soldiers, they weren't scared. It was reassuring, one woman said, to think that the might of the Army had come to help them. They were to leave for a few days, the loudspeakers said, just as a precaution, so the scientists could do tests and the firemen could wash down the roads and buildings. They were to take with them essential documents only – identity cards and papers, marriage and birth certificates – and schoolchildren could bring their books, but that was all. Even now, the women said, no one was scared, or if they were, they were just beginning to be. They talked of leaving bread on the table, and spoons – old folks' superstitions, at their mother-in-law's or grandmother's insistence. If there is bread on the table, and a spoon for every soul in the house, then you can come back, and things will be as they were. Some of them – their stories started to fragment now – suspected that something was wrong, and they tried to smuggle out belongings by wearing three dresses over each other, wrapping their babies in extra blankets and hiding in the layers valuables like silver christening spoons, putting seed potatoes in their children's pockets and hoods. But the soldiers knew, and the soldiers stopped them. Some tried to bring their cats, or the best-laying hens, and were forced at gunpoint to abandon them. Children were crying by now, and some old babushkas were refusing to leave, accusing the government of trying to steal their cow, their goat, their silver, sitting down in the middle of the road or running into the forest, and the soldiers dragged them up and slung them into the army trucks like sacks of manure.

I'm going into too much detail. This was only the backdrop, so to speak: it isn't the important part, the part I need to tell. That part came next.

As the chorus of women started telling of the evacuation and subsequent days and weeks, the camp beds in school gymnasiums and allocation of rooms in damp tower blocks, the fear and rumours that bred from each other, especially once the sickness started, the nausea and vomiting and diarrhoea that affected most of them, but the children and infants worst, the blister packs of iodine tablets and half-gallons of milk distributed to each head of household, the hair loss and weight loss and ulcerated skin, the doctors who wore rubber suits and masks even when weighing and examining babies – as they spoke of these things, they grew visibly more upset until one by one they refused to talk any more. They got up and walked away or turned their faces from the camera, until the documentary cut to a picture of a graveyard and a voice-over began about mortality rates and radiation sickness in children.

Then a new story began. Compared to this story, the Pripyat survivors' tales paled. You understood they'd been – pardon the grotesque phrase, but this is what it seemed like – a sort of warm-up act.

The second story took the angle of the workers at the plant, the ones who'd been there on that Friday. Most if not all of them were dead, the voiceover intoned; they'd died within weeks. The documentary crew had been unable to track down many surviving relatives who were prepared to talk to a camera: the narrator hinted at obstruction by politicians, and veiled threats, and thwarted leads. This was, as he reminded us, little more than a decade after the incident. But they'd found one widow, Nastasya, they called her, although that wasn't her real name. She sat in profile to the camera, so that most of her face was in shadow. Her black headscarf was tightly bound under her chin, and her voice, in the gaps between the translation, was low and rasping. On the day of the explosions, she was twenty-two, and she had been married for three months and seventeen days. I could tell you the hours, too, she said. I could tell you the minutes and the seconds, because we were newlyweds, and each hour and minute and second was a kind of wonder. We said *I love you* many times a day, and I think now that we didn't know what those words meant. Her husband was a worker at the plant, she said, and they lived in the dormitory with the other workers and wives, a seven-storey block about half a mile from Chernobyl. Their room was on the fourth floor, facing north, and when they heard the blasts they got up and went to the window – it was about half past one in the morning – and they could see the flames. Her husband, Aleksander, was working the early shift, from six to six, and she tried to persuade him to come back to bed, but he was already buttoning on his shirt and overalls and said that it was his duty to help, they had been drilled for this, she must go back to bed and keep all the windows closed.

The day passed, and he didn't come home, and she and the other wives watched the flames in the sky and could feel the heat of them. Then six o'clock passed, the time when his shift should have ended, had he been working a regular shift, and still nothing, and some of the wives were worried now because their husbands had been gone for twenty-four hours. Word went around that the fire was worse than expected and that men from the plant had been taken to hospital. A group of wives set off for the hospital but the roads were cordoned off and the police weren't letting anyone through. Some women begged, and others tried to bribe the policemen, and in the confusion two of them got through, Nastasya and one other. The other woman had a brother-in-law who was an orderly at the hospital and he took the women to the ward and they saw their husbands – so red and swollen their mouths and eyes had vanished in their faces. While they were there, one of the men – there were about fifteen of them, she guessed, in that room anyhow – one of them vomited a great gush of blood and died. They knew then that the men had been poisoned: by gas, people were saying, by fumes from the smoke, and the orderly was yelling at them to get out, and saying that if they wanted to help they could bring milk. Milk? Yes, milk, the men needed milk, they needed to drink as much milk as possible, and the hospital couldn't provide it, or couldn't provide enough. So she and the other woman left and rushed to the nearest store and bought as much milk as they could carry: but by the time they got back to the hospital the crowd of people there – mainly wives and mothers of the hospitalised workers – had doubled, and the cordon had been strengthened, there were soldiers there by now, and military vehicles, and there was no way of getting through. People were yelling and shoving and clawing one another and wailing and the containers of milk got lost, trampled and split underfoot. A soldier announced through a megaphone that the Army was airlifting the men to hospital in Moscow, where there were better facilities and more doctors, and each man would need a change of clothes and some food for the journey, strictly limited to one bag per patient, and would be allowed to see his wife or mother for five minutes when it was handed over. So all of the women rushed back to their dormitories or flats but by the time they came back with their bundle of clothes – their husband's or son's smartest suit and shoes, a clean shirt and necktie, because they weren't going to have their men looked down on in the city – and their string bag with a stoppered bottle of milk, a hunk of black bread and cheese, perhaps a hip flask of spirits, whatever they could lay their hands on: they realised that the Army had tricked them and the men were gone, loaded straight from their beds onto military aircraft, the orderlies said.

Can you even begin to imagine?

Not all of the women were able to follow their husbands and sons to Moscow. Many of them had babies or young children, elderly parents; many of them had never left their villages, were scared. But Nastasya went, and two others, pawning their gold rings and best shoes for the airfare.

In Moscow, it took two days of begging and bribing before they found out the name of the hospital – it was a special hospital, for radiology, on the outskirts of the city – and another day before they persuaded a receptionist to let them in. The head doctor wouldn't let them up at first – oh, the agony, knowing that their husbands were metres away from them – but eventually she relented and said they could have twenty minutes, but they must keep two metres away at all times; no touching, and certainly no kissing.

Nastasya laughed when she said this. How do you expect, she said, turning towards the camera for the first time, that a woman will stay two metres from her beloved and not kiss him? As for the twenty minutes: now that she had found him, her Aleksy, she wasn't going to leave him again, ever.

How do you find the strength to tell a story like that? How do you find the strength to live it?

Nastasya's voice grows harsh and proud as she tells of how she stayed near her husband. Many of the doctors and orderlies were mutinying, refusing to work the Chernobyl ward, or simply not turning up to work at all, scared of the clicking Geiger counters and the masks they were given to wear. So Nastasya and the other women took over the duties, carrying trays of food, emptying bedpans, and in this way they managed to stay close to their husbands. Each day, she said, there were more dead, and each day her Aleksander had died a little, too. If you spill boiling water or borscht or hot oil on your skin, or go too close to a normal flame, it burns from the outside in. But his body had been burned deep on the inside, a doctor explained, and as the burns came to the surface his skin peeled away in layers, first patches the size of a small coin, then saucers, and then sections the size of a plate, leaving lesions behind, raw flesh that smelled as if it was cooking. His teeth loosened and came out as he coughed or talked – he spat them in clumps of bone and gum into his hand. His hair rubbed off in handfuls as she stroked it. He was shitting blood and mucus twenty, thirty times a day, and parts of his intestines, coiled in on themselves, were coming out, too. His pupils were like a dead rabbit's, swollen and glazed. The head doctor begged her to leave. He is no longer your husband, she said. He is a dangerous radioactive object. Go. Save yourself. It is what he would want, surely? But I couldn't go, she says. How could I go? How could I leave him? In his brief periods of sentience, he clutched at her hand and tried to form his mouth into the shape of her name. He knew who she was, he knew she was there: how could she leave him? In the last days, he was coughing up parts of his internal organs – chunks of liver, slimy and blackened – and she had to pluck them from his mouth with her fingers. No doctors by then would go near him.

She stops talking for a long moment.

When he died, she says, they wouldn't give me his body. They said it had to be buried in a lead-lined coffin, in a place far from anywhere anyone might ever go.

Will you find out? she says, turning straight towards the camera and interviewer. Will you find out where they have buried my husband, so I can lie beside him?

I have three different types of cancer, she says, but the cancers are not going to get me until I have found Aleksander Alexeivich.

At this point the off-camera interviewer asks her something, in a murmur.

And she turns again, straight to the camera, and says in broken, heavily accented English: Why I do it? If you need to ask this, then you are stupid, you are foolish old woman, and I would not trade my life and health for yours, even now. Why I do it? Because I love him, is why. Because is what love is.

I didn't see the end of it. Five minutes or so of summary, I imagine there must have been, to take it up to the end of the hour. I fumbled for the remote control and managed to switch it off, the screen closing over Nastasya's pale, twisted, transfigured face, and I sat there, trembling. Trembling is the right word: ripples of it were racing through and over my whole body. Something I hadn't known had been thickening in me up to that moment, until Nastasya and her Aleksander dragged it to the surface. It was the realisation that if my mother had watched Nastasya talking of her sweetheart, she would have understood. She would have had a level of pity or compassion or understanding or whatever the word might be that surpassed the gruesome, car-crash compulsion of the story. Because she loved my father. She would have done what Nastasya did, for him. In fact, in a way, what she did was exactly that. I suddenly remembered her saying, and it was as clearly as if she was right beside me, speaking the words again now, *I would do it all again, I wouldn't trade anything, not even the outcome, not even if I knew the outcome right from the start.* She'd said it after the funeral, when we were doorstepped, and it had been printed in the trashier papers, large, in capital letters. And I realised how much there was that I didn't understand, that I'd never asked, and never could ask now. Our mother rarely talked about our father: she kept him all shut up inside of her, as if in talking of him she'd disperse him, or leak her store of him away. Towards the end I tried to ask her, but she wouldn't answer; when she did talk, it was loose and rambling, and made little or no sense. I'd gone through her things after she died, and even the shoeboxed scraps of memento she had – the odd photo or bus ticket, cinema stub or hospital wristband, cassette tape or electricity bill, old airline tickets from the days when you had actual tickets, postcards, perforated strips of negatives, a copy of Sylvia Plath's *Winter Trees* (she'd asked for that, in hospital, and we hadn't been able to find it, and only found it afterwards) – none of them meant anything, none of them told me anything about her, or about him. A lot of them, I couldn't work out if she'd kept out of sentiment or in a slow drift of accumulation, never getting round to throwing them away.

I have the boxes here, *Clarks* and *Dolcis* and one *Russell & Bromley*, stacked up beside the sofa, because I couldn't bring myself to throw them away, either.

It's almost unbearable, the feeling that you've never really known someone, after all, and that now your chance to know them is gone.

So that's what this is. On Tuesday 29th March 2011, I am beginning my attempt to tell my story, and set the past to rights and to rest, and to understand.

I suppose I'd better begin at the beginning. Perhaps I should have done that all along. Ignored this documentary, and its effect on things. Or summarised it more briefly. For one thing, it's gruesome using real people's lives, real people's deaths, to try and explain something of mine, I know. The scales of suffering are incomparable. All I can say is that even though I can't quite articulate why exactly it's important, I just know it is, crucially so. In my defence, I have tried not to linger, or to be gratuitous. If you ever watch it for yourself, you will see that: you will see that it is hundreds of times more terrible and more harrowing in the flesh than in my words. But I am trying to be truthful – there's no point in doing any of this if I'm not truthful – and telling the truth, somehow getting to the truth, or towards it, is the only thing that seems to matter. For my life was a whole tissue of deception and lies.

The beginning, as you will see, was in many ways the ending of everything, too.

THE MEMOIRS OF LARA MOORHOUSE

Fuengirola

We went on holiday only once as a family. July 1985, Fuengirola, on the Costa del Sol in Spain. I turned twelve that summer – in fact, I had my twelfth birthday while we were there. It was the moment everything began to fall apart.

Alfie – who would have been seven and a half – and I were of course wildly excited about the trip from the moment our father first announced it to us. For days afterwards, we talked of nothing else. I remember one afternoon in particular, jumping around the living room listing the firsts. It was our first time on an aeroplane, our first time out of England – except it actually wasn't, I suddenly pointed out, with all the self-righteous pedantry of an older sister. Belfast, technically, was in a different country than England. A different island, anyhow, and a place you had either to fly or get the ferry to definitely counted as 'out of England'. And I'd been there, and Alfie hadn't, and so although it was his first time out of England, it was my second.

Our mother must have overheard our squabbles because next thing I knew I was being yanked up by the arm – we'd been on our bellies on the brown and orange living-room rug, consulting a map of the world as I proved to Alfie I was right – and she had me by the shoulders, gripping them so tightly it hurt, and shaking me a little. Her face was inches from mine as she shouted, and I could see the places where her brown lipstick bled into the tiny gullies and wrinkles around her lips.

'Do you hear me?' she was shouting. I didn't: I was too shocked and surprised to take in what was happening. My mother was small, and slight, and self-contained. I struggle to remember more than a handful of occasions when she raised her voice at us and I don't think she hit either of us even once. She was named after Jane Eyre in her mother's favourite novel, and the family joke – she told this to me, once, in an unguarded moment, and I never forgot it – was that she was as quiet and plain and shy as her namesake. This behaviour – wrenching at my arm, physically hurting me, yelling right in my face – was so completely out of character that I froze, went numb. I was as nonplussed, I think, as I was scared. I could not for the life of me work out what was wrong: what I could possibly have done.

'You're hurting me,' I managed. An ugly mauve bloom had spread up my mother's neck and into her cheeks and I could see it crawling through her temples and into her scalp. She suddenly loosened her grip – her hands went limp and fell by her sides – and I took a step back. We stared at each other for a moment and then, without taking her eyes from me, she said, 'Go to your bedroom, Alfie.'

He turned and scuttled from the room.

'You must never,' she said, 'and I mean *never* – do you hear me? – repeat again that you've been to Ireland. Not to Alfie, not to anyone. Not even to me, and certainly not to Daddy. Do you hear me, Lara?'

I said I did.

'You promise me?' she went on.

'I promise,' I said, and I think I was very probably on the brink of tears by now because she reached for my hand, gently this time, and sat us both down on the sofa.

'I'm sorry, petal,' she said. 'I scared you, didn't I? I didn't mean to. I just – didn't think you remembered, that's all.'

She was stroking my hand, pulling and massaging at the fingers, as she sometimes did, and I wished she'd let go of it.

'Why is it' – I tried to frame the question in a way that wouldn't make her explode again – 'why does it – I mean . . .' I trailed off.

'When you're a little bit older,' she said, and even counting everything that happened afterwards, it's the saddest I've ever seen her, ever. 'When you and Alfie are both a bit older, then you'll understand.'

It was she who looked old, suddenly. In less than the time it took her to say those words, she had aged centuries, millennia, and I felt a gulf between us, an abyss, that could never be bridged. A child should never see the depths of its parent's sorrow. You can never forget it, once you've seen something like that: it is irrevocable.

She'd left off rubbing at my hand, and even though only a moment ago I'd been willing her to stop, I couldn't bear it now that she had. I nudged her hand with mine and when she didn't respond I picked up her right hand with my left and clumsily worked the fingers for her.

'It's OK, Mummy,' I said, using the childish name I'd lately stopped using. 'It's OK. You don't have to explain.

You never have to explain anything.' I meant it, too: I meant it with every desperate, straining atom of my heart. So long as she was all right again, and we could pretend it hadn't happened – I was furiously, silently bargaining with her, with myself – I wouldn't ever ask her, would never do anything that might again bring that haunted, beyond-wretched look into her eyes. I nuzzled my head against her, into the space between her neck and shoulder. I kissed behind her ears again and again with the soft little kisses we used to call 'fairy kisses' and I promised her that I would never mention Ireland again and I'd forget, I would, I promise, cross my heart and hope to die, that we'd ever been there.

It was raining in London on the day we set off for Fuengirola. Rather than dampening our spirits – and it was a heavy rainstorm, soaking our feet in their stiff new sandals and spattering with liquid London pavement the new spaghetti-strapped white dress that I'd insisted on wearing – the weather made us even more gleeful. The incident with my mother would have been around Easter time, I think, and by the time summer came I must have been genuinely excited again. There would have been more than two months for the anticipation to build: two busy months in which there were passports to apply for, swimming costumes and sundresses and sandals to buy, different suntan lotions and cool-smelling aftersuns to study in the chemist's. Besides, even if it wasn't my first time 'out of England' it was still my first proper holiday, and first time flying, and our first holiday as a family longer than a weekend in Brighton or the Suffolk coast.

I remember repeating to myself, like a mantra, *We're all going on a summer holiday*, and even now I have to flip the radio station or leave the room if that wretched song comes on. So when the day finally arrived Alfie and I capered and squealed down the street, tugging and bumping our new suitcases, revelling in the looks of annoyance from passers-by. The prospect of being on the beach in the Costa del Sol by that very afternoon was made even sweeter by the fact that we should have been in school: it was a Monday, I seem to remember, and there was at least a week before we broke up for the holidays. I don't know how our mother had managed to persuade the head teacher to let us miss the end of term, and I remember my class teacher, fat old Mrs Ingle, wasn't pleased about it at all.

I've been staring at those last sentences for almost ten minutes now, seized, riddled with doubts. Was I really content to be missing the end of the school year? It was my last year of primary school, after all, and although the majority of my classmates, myself included, were going on to the same local secondary school, a significant number weren't, and so the last days were to be filled with goodbye parties culminating in a grand prize-giving and 'graduation' ceremony complete with playlets that we'd written and been rehearsing ourselves. The force with which those memories come back to me, almost thirty years later, suggests that deep down, I must have felt that I was missing out – or at the very least, that I wasn't as carelessly happy as it might have seemed. Perhaps my hysteria and general capering, unlike Alfie's, was part of an act: a show for my mother, who ever since the Ireland incident had been strained, nervous, somehow not-quite-right. Or perhaps it was me who was different: even if I was oblivious when it happened, I wasn't afterwards. I'd begun, against my will, to notice things that I hadn't noticed before, begun to watch my mother – and my father, but especially my mother – carefully, when I thought she wouldn't know, tracking her moods and expressions and nuances of her speech. Perhaps it was myself I was trying to fool, not her. How to know? A handful of pages in, and already it seems that it's going to be impossible to get inside the past, to really be true to it. We can only see it from the outside, squinting back at it, and it changes utterly depending on the mood and circumstances and point from which we happen to be regarding it. There is no one meaning, no correct or tidy interpretation, only a maybe-this, a what-if-that. I didn't know this before. I look back at what I have written so far and it is a halting, juddering hotchpotch of perhaps, but, perhaps. I will try to be bolder. If it weren't for the fact that the events of this story would seem impossible, too lurid to be true, I might try to write it as fiction. You have none of these hideous doubts in fiction: you are completely in control of your characters. There's none of the doubt or hedging that comes from trying to be real and true. But as I've said already, there are too many lies already in my story.

So: Fuengirola. My mother got drunk on the plane. My mother rarely drank, and never drank alone: only when our father was there, to keep him company. She always had a bottle of red wine in the house, and a bottle of his favourite whiskey (a variety of Bushmills called 'Black Bush'), but they were for him, in case his schedule changed and he came home unannounced or unexpectedly, as he sometimes did. I never once saw her touch them without him. On the plane, though, she got drunk, ordering one gin-and-tonic after another, upending the little green bottle over the ice and splashing in the tonic with shaking hands, then downing the entire thing in three or four swallows. For the first gin-and-tonic, she made a stilted joke to the air hostess that we'd already set our watches to Spanish time, which was an hour ahead, so it was 'p.m.' and therefore respectable. She was too apologetic: I cringed. Other passengers seated just ahead of us had asked for gin-and-tonics, or miniature bottles of vodka and whisky: she didn't need to explain, and explaining just drew attention to it. She dropped the pretence at a joke with the second, and the third she leaned into the aisle to pluck from the trolley herself. I was mortified. I shrank down in my seat and tried to read *Harriet the Spy*, but it was no use. All I could hear was the sound of my mother ripping the foil packets of nuts with her teeth and pouring the whole contents into her mouth, scrunching up the packet in her palm and a minute later unclenching her hand, flattening the foil out and folding it up neatly into itself, a stiff little triangle, then picking at it until it came loose. Or fiddling with her wedding ring – a pretty, silver 'lover's knot' of the sort that had three rings intertwined in one, which she sometimes let me play with. Twisting it round and round, rolling it up to the joint of her finger and back down to the knuckle, until I wanted to slap her hands down still. She had a new book for the journey, a fat paperback in the sorts of colours she never let herself read, but she didn't so much as open it. She didn't eat her meal: the perfect little breast of chicken on a circle of buttery mash, the square of green beans and the bread roll and the chocolate éclair, each in its own neat foil container, and with every bite that I ate and she didn't I tasted the grim, gin-soaked despair of her mood. She hadn't taken off her sunglasses, either. Alfie and I, as I've said, had insisted on wearing our new clothes to the airport – my white sundress embroidered with red cherries and his sky-blue shorts and the shirt with the appliquéd parrot on it – and we both had on our Mickey Mouse sunglasses and hats, mine a floppy woven one with a brim, his a baseball cap on backwards. So it hadn't seemed strange when our mother appeared from her bedroom in her sunglasses, and kept them on even underground on the Tube, and inside the airport. In the excitement of gazing at the flashing board of destinations, hearing the announcements of exotic locations and imminent departures, pressing our noses to the thick, smeared glass of the terminal wall to watch the aeroplanes swooping up and nose-diving down, we didn't notice that she hadn't taken them off. Now, I noticed. Alfie, torn between his new *Beano* and looking out of the window, didn't notice a thing. I accepted the boiled ginger sucky sweet the air hostess gave me and then buried my nose in the paper sick bag.

It was Alfie who saw our father first: the minute we walked down the metal staircase and onto the tarmac of the runway, into the strange, thick, sweet-smelling heat of the Spanish afternoon. Our father was at the window of the terminal building, wearing a cowboy hat and waving. Alfie yelled and started to wave and run towards him, weaving through the lumbering line of people, white legs and slapping sandals. Our mother had stopped, to the annoyance of the people behind us, and was looking up sharply to where Alfie had pointed, biting her freshly fuchsiaed bottom lip, holding her sunglasses down and squinting against the sun.

'He's here,' she said aloud, though not to me, and that was another clue I registered, though didn't understand: because why wouldn't he be there?

My father, I should probably explain at this point, was a doctor, a plastic surgeon, and he worked a lot of the time in Northern Ireland. There was a great need for surgeons there, on account of the 'Troubles', the bombs and kneecappings you sometimes saw on the news, and which our mother always turned off. He was flying out to Malaga directly from Belfast, and would meet us at the airport that afternoon; that was the plan.

'He's here,' she said again, and she took my hand then and we walked into the terminal. I remember she was singing some silly song – what it was I don't recall, but I am sure that she was singing. It was the first time all day I'd seen her relaxed, seen something of her normal self. It was the only time, those long, impatient twenty minutes or so we waited for our bags before going through into the Arrivals hall. Because when we went through, he wasn't there.

We saw the man who was meant to be him. Close-up, he looked nothing like our dad. He was the same height, and the same general sort of shape, but his face – which had been hidden by the brim of the cowboy hat – bore no similarity at all to our father's. Our mother went very silent, and very still. I turned and shouted at Alfie: how could he have been so stupid, our father didn't even have a cowboy hat, had we in our entire lives ever seen him in a cowboy hat, or any hat at all? Alfie cowered; he was confused, his round blue eyes filling up with tears as he looked between me and the man who wasn't our father, and I wanted to thump him, to kick him, to mash him into a pulp. Poor Alfie. I'm ashamed to admit it, but I almost did. I lifted my arm, hand fisted, ready to punch him, and it was that which spurred our mother into action. She seized my arm and lowered it and pushed me in the direction of a bank of plastic chairs. Then she took Alfie's hand – he was crying by now, tears and snot slugging down his cheeks – and heaved our suitcases over to the chairs.

'What are we going to do?' I asked.

She looked at me as if I was a stranger. 'We wait.'

'Where's Daddy?' Alfie sobbed.

At this point a Spanish woman, who must have witnessed the scene, came over. She asked, in accented English, if she could help.

'No, thank you,' our mother said, and stared straight ahead.

The Spanish woman was friendly, with an open face and kind eyes, and I felt embarrassed at my mother's rudeness.

'We're waiting for my father,' I said. 'He was supposed to be here already, he was on a flight earlier than ours, but he isn't here.'

'Lara,' my mother said, in a voice that would have sounded quiet from the outside.

'Oh, but that is terrible,' the Spanish woman was saying, and she motioned over a boy – her son, I assume – who was standing a little distance away. 'What flight was your husband on?' she said to my mother, 'we will check with airport information if it has been delayed or if perhaps your husband missed it.'

'It's quite all right,' my mother said, icy. 'We don't need your help.'

'Belfast,' I blurted out.

My mother gazed at me as if I'd committed the worst possible betrayal. I didn't care. I went on. 'He was flying out from Belfast this morning.'

'Belfast, eh?' the woman said, turning to me now. 'You have the flight number?'

I shook my head. The woman spoke a stream of rapid Spanish to her son.

My mother stood up. 'How many times,' she began, and her voice was thin with rage, 'do I have to tell you that we don't want, or need, your assistance?' The woman blinked at her. 'My children,' she went on, 'are overexcited and overtired. They misunderstood when I told them that their father would meet us at the airport. In fact, we have to wait a while here, and he will pick us up from the airport. That is all. There is no disaster, no mystery.' She paused; eyeballed the woman through her big blank sunglasses. She still hadn't taken them off. 'Thank you for your concern.'

There was a short silence. The woman looked from my mother to me, to us, and back to her son. He was sixteen or seventeen, maybe, with lanky hair in a rat's-tail plait at the back of his neck and boils like raspberries on his neck and face. He was embarrassed. He muttered something in Spanish. She snapped something back.

'Well,' she said, and she said a word or so in Spanish, and then they turned and walked away.

Neither Alfie nor I dared say anything. We had never seen our mother behave like this before. We sat on the glossy moulded chairs, and waited.

He didn't come, he didn't come, he didn't come. Alfie, too scared to ask for permission to move, wet himself. It seeped down his shorts in a darkening stain and trickled down his leg. You could smell it, too, after a while. Our mother, straight-backed and still, didn't notice. I pretended I didn't, either.

I watched the surges of people coming through the Arrivals gate. The milk-bottle legs and arms of English families on package tours, new sandals already rubbing heels raw. The Spanish couples reuniting. An occasional businessman, dark-haired and sunglassed. I watched through the crowds for our father, his big, square, handsome face which would be head-and-shoulders above the rest. Sometimes, for a split second, I almost thought I saw him, the shape of his back, or heard the sound of his voice. There were too many greetings in the air, and they all grated. After each influx of people, I trained my eyes on the exits, flicking between both of them in case, as our mother had said, he was coming to pick us up rather than meet us at the airport. I don't know why she had lied. I knew the plan: I had heard them making it. He would be there when we got there, I had heard him say it, those exact words.

The trickle of water left in my flask was warm and tasted like saliva. I needed the toilet, too, and despite myself, my stomach was rumbling. We had been waiting for almost two hours, now.

At six o'clock precisely – she must have been waiting for the hour, giving him ten more minutes, five, one more minute – our mother stood up and said that he wasn't coming. We would get a taxi to the complex instead, she said. Alfie and I panicked. How would he know, we said, that we'd gone on? What if something had happened to him? But our mother ignored our flurry of questions.

'Come on,' she said, and she picked up her suitcase and Alfie's and started walking, which left us with no choice but to do the same. She had an envelope of pesetas – emergency money – in her jacket, which would be enough to get us there and to last a day or so. Our father would come when he came. Despite everything, something about her strange calmness, her practicality, quietened us. We trotted along after her and didn't argue any more.

I remember very little about the taxi ride beyond my bursting bladder. It wasn't a long journey – half an hour or so – but I have never felt so scared or helpless, rushing through the evening, the window jammed down and the warm Spanish breeze tangling my hair across my face, the driver's techno music on loud, everything foreign, everything wrong.

When we reached the outskirts of Fuengirola and had been unloaded outside the reception of the complex we were staying in, I dashed to the toilet. When I came out, we had been checked in and had the keys to our apartment, and my mother was smiling strangely. Our father had left a message, she said, with the woman at reception. It was written in badly spelled biro on the back of an old invoice. He had been unable to meet us, it said, he was sorry, there had been complications in the journey. He hoped to get to us tomorrow, perhaps the next day. We were to check in, relax, enjoy ourselves. Our mother was to be at the telephone in reception at nine the next morning and he would call her then.

Everything should have been all right then, but it wasn't; we were too exhausted and wound-up for that. We trailed after our mother and the woman from reception as she took us around the complex and showed us into our ground-floor apartment, one of about fifty built in steep white tiers like a wedding cake. There was a big swimming pool, built like a number eight, the top part a shallow children's pool and the larger bottom half a deeper pool for adults, with a concrete bridge in the middle, like a belt –

Writing that, I'm suddenly reminded of Alfie's favourite joke of the time: 'What did the zero say to the 8? Nice belt!' I remember how his favourite book was a paperback called something like *Ha-Ha Bonk*, a compendium for children. 'What did the traffic light say to the car? Don't look now, I'm changing!' and 'Doctor, Doctor, people keep ignoring me. Next, please!' and 'How did the monkey make toast? He put his bread under the gorilla!' The book had been one of our father's Thursday presents

– Thursday being the day he most often arrived home from his work in Ireland – and Alfie read it from cover to cover and back again until he had memorised the jokes for Dad, laboriously. He was a slow reader and bad speller, and frequently had to ask our mother or me what a joke meant and why it was funny. I can see him now, his pinched, thin little face, pale eyebrows scrunched, peering through the side rail on the top bunk bed and trying to understand the pun on 'grill' and 'gorilla'. This isn't relevant, really, to the story I'm telling – or at least to the Fuengirola thread that I'm following right now. But it seems to me that in too many books people's memories come in seamless waves, perfectly coherent and lyrical. Recollections come like that one just did to me, searing, intense and jagged from nowhere, burning bright when before there was nothing. I could delete this and go on with the story, picking up from where the woman showed us into our apartment. *We didn't even fight over beds. We just sat down, not looking at each other, and began the wait for Dad.* But it feels somehow right to keep it in, meaningless detail though it is. It isn't important in the way the Chernobyl documentary is important: rather it seems like something semi-precious, something I didn't have until the writing itself summoned it up for me, like a ghost of itself. Ahlberg. Janet and Allan Ahlberg, who wrote as well as the joke compendium the baby books we loved so much, and the one about the cops and robbers. Our father read us that book. I can see him, now, and hear him, too, the rhythms and rhymes pulled like toffee in his gritty-then-soft Belfast accent. I didn't realise I remembered. I didn't realise I'd forgotten. His voice is there, out of nowhere, right inside my head, as real as if I'm actually hearing it. How strange that voices, or the memory of them, can be preserved intact, caught out of the medium in which they exist, echoing suddenly in the hidden chambers of our minds or hearts.

And all of a sudden I find I don't want to write any more, about my father, about what has to happen next.

Brompton Cemetery

The start of May, the sky a deep, sure blue. I have today off, after working over the bank holiday weekend. I meant to sleep in, but the pigeons bumping and scraping and chittering on the ledge above my window woke me up at the usual time, just before seven. The room was airless, and the light already too bright for the thin blinds to be effective. When you inch open the window, pigeon fluff and dried-up scrags of pavement grime come wafting in, and the smell, and the clattering of footsteps on the metal plate above. So I got up and came here, Brompton Cemetery, with a takeaway coffee and my notebook.

I didn't know I was coming here until I realised I was walking on past Hammersmith, past the Charing Cross Hospital and down the Fulham Road, left into Lillie Road, past Normand Park: down all of the old streets. I think I thought I was headed for the river, to walk the Mall for a while. Watch the morning rowers hauling upstream and skimming back, or the salvage-collectors, trudging through the stinking mudflats with their thigh-high waders and their hooked sticks and sacks. Find a bench and listen to the seagulls, marvel – I always do – at how curved and cruel their beaks are, how blank and beady their eyes, how big they are when they jump up close. Maybe go as far out as Chiswick, the story-book houses with rambling roses up their painted porches, the private locked gardens at the water's edge, Chiswick Eyot, the tiny tidal island, where a man is supposed to have lived until recently. Lately, or at least since Jeremy, this is how I have been spending my days off. It's somehow soothing walking the river: the routine of it, the fact that it's always and never the same. Instead, here I seem to have come, Brompton Cemetery, not entirely of my own – at least conscious – accord.

It's been more than a month since I started writing about the holiday in Fuengirola. So many memories came back so vivid and painful I thought I couldn't bear it. I've carried on taking Mr Rawalpindi to the Monday night classes at the Irish Cultural Centre – which is what made the idea of writing my story seem possible – but I've sat at the back and not made any notes, and when the teacher took me aside one break-time and asked if everything was all right I just shrugged and said *I* wasn't here to write, I was just the carer. I vowed I wouldn't write again. When I made all the grandiose resolutions after *The Chernobyl Effect*, the panicked scrabbling belief that telling my story would save my life – what was I thinking? How embarrassing to think how desperate and earnest I was. I was just overwrought. As if a story can save you: ridiculous, I know now, in the light of day. Yet here I am, notebook in hand, readying myself to write some more. As if it's brimmed up in me until it's going to spill over, and I have no choice but to catch it. Or as if once unleashed, the memories aren't going to go away: so I must write them down, pin them, trap them into chains of words so they can't flap around my head at night and haunt me.

It's been a while since I came here – perhaps even years, I don't remember – but the place never changes. Just as we did when we were little, I have it almost to my-self, on this anonymous Tuesday morning. Apart from the gay men cruising – mostly foreigners, Italian-looking, in mirrored sunglasses and their tightest shiny shirts. I'm sure there weren't so many of them in those days, or they were more furtive, or perhaps we just didn't notice them. The worlds of adults and children, coexisting, overlap-ping and overlaid, but impervious to each other.

Brompton Cemetery: we used to come here to play, Alfie and I, summer evenings and Saturdays and during school holidays. Dad would fly back on a Thursday morning, not every Thursday, but at least every fortnight, and he'd usually have the weekend, until Sunday lunch-time, although sometimes things were so bad in North-ern Ireland that he'd be needed straight back, on the early Saturday flight. Thursday was his consultation day, I think, and Fridays were usually surgery. I wish I knew more of the details: but when you're a child, you're only vaguely interested in what your father does. If there were complications – something not healing properly, or something needing an eye kept on – he'd stay on a few extra days, and we longed for this, though it rarely happened. The complicated procedures, the ones that re-quired him to be there for aftercare and that couldn't be handed over to the clinic's nurses and permanent staff, he did in August, or over Easter, times when he'd stay home for a fortnight or more. His clinic was one of the best on Harley Street and it was stuffed with surgeons and private nurses. A lot of them, like him, worked part of the week elsewhere and took private clients at the clinic on a part-time basis. I remember my mother saying, once, that Belfast surgeons were regarded as the best in the world. It was on account of the practice they had, with gunshot and baseball-bat and bomb-blast victims, though of course we didn't know this then. But we did know that if you needed private cosmetic work done – your nose straightened or thinned, your brow tightened, the new face-lifting techniques – you came to Harley Street and asked for a Belfast surgeon.

In the midst of all this – shuttling between Belfast and London, the Troubles, the pressures of private practice – it's only understandable that he craved time alone with our mother. So he'd give us some money, enough for the bus fare and the cinema if it was rainy, or else for a king's ransom of sweets and comics at Mr Patel's. That's what he always called it, 'a king's ransom'. He had an eloquent way of talking, our father: like something out of a story. The gift of the gab. On dry days we'd pile our pockets with Refresher bars – those were Alfie's favourites – and Curly Wurlys (mine) and walk the short distance from our flat to the North Gate of the Cemetery, where Eardley Crescent meets the Old Brompton Road. It may sound strange, if you don't know the place, to think of children being sent off to play in a cemetery. We loved it. This was our playground, the set for our elaborate adventures, inspiration for the ghost stories I used to make up for Alfie. There were endless games to be played: racing along these colonnades, hiding behind the tombstones and mausoleums, trying to tame a robin or a squirrel. Searching for the grave of the famous Red

Indian Chief Long Wolf, who died here when he was taking part in Buffalo Bill's Wild West Show. Competitions to find the oldest person, or the youngest. Alice McKenzie, who lived to be one hundred and one, from 1852 to 1953. Little Rose Eliza Gray, who lasted less than six months in 1897. I remember them without even having to look for the graves. The legions of young men killed in the Charge of the Light Brigade, the sorrowful memorials for those 'Killed in Action', whose bodies lie unmarked in Lempire or the Somme. We were fascinated by those. I think that the only way Alfie learned to read at all – because he was so slow at school, always – was by my helping him to pick out names and dates on the tombstones.

It wasn't morbid, is what I suppose I'm trying to say. We were happy here. On home-game Saturdays we used to sit under the East Stand of Stamford Bridge, which rises like a metal spider up behind the catacombs and mock Basilica, and try to guess the score by the roars of the crowd and the songs they were singing. I'd make bets with Alfie on which player had scored, or almost scored, and I used to tease him until he was tormented. Poor Alfie: it was the closest he ever got to seeing his team play. Our mother despised football, and Dad followed Man United. That was always an agony for Alfie, being torn between the team all his friends supported – the team whose stadium he could almost see from our flat – and the club his father followed. They weren't then the arch-rivals they are now, but even so. Dad bought him a Man Utd football shirt once, for a birthday, I think. It had *George Best* on the back. Alfie never wore it out, apart from that one time he put it on to show Dad, just after he'd unwrapped it. To make things even worse than the fact it was a Man U shirt, George Best had gone on to play for Fulham, our hated rivals. Alfie used to worry that Dad would realise he never wore it – he was an awful worrier, Alfie – but Dad never did. After he died, Alfie wore it in bed instead of his pyjamas until our mother said it was unhygienic. After that it disappeared.

So many memories, spilling back, cramming in on top of each other, sparking each other, jostling. And now. Coming up for midday, and the same dappled sunlight and flittering shadows, the same overgrowth of nettles, dandelion clocks and long lush grasses, the same lacy reek of cow parsley, sweet smell of clover. Sitting here at the end of the colonnade, my back against the warm stone, listening to the grass ticking with insects and to the birdsong, it could almost be then, worlds overlaid again. The same blackbird I'm watching hop from gravestone to sinking gravestone, the same fluffed-up preening wood pigeons splashing in the puddle under the water fountain's tap. If I don't turn around, it suddenly seems I might feel myself run past, the wake of me, plimsolled feet slapping and skidding along the flagstones, breathless and laughing as I turn at the end and hurtle back.

Words are treacherous. I see why people have always feared them and feared those who could use them; in ages past seen their use as a black art. Writing about the Chernobyl documentary filled me with a strange, wild fear – and power. Writing about Fuengirola called all sorts of things, not all of them happy, few of them welcome, into being. As I wrote those sentences above, as I read them back to myself, it feels as if I have the power to be summoning myself back. I know there's nothing, nobody, in the archway behind me but I am half-afraid to turn around to see. Afraid that my ten-year-old self will be there, afraid again that she won't.

If I was a witch or a shaman, used to travelling between worlds – last night's late-night TV – I would have talismans, tokens, things to attach me to the real world, to bring me back if I got lost. Stones or beads or amulets, feathers or figurines. What I have is a cup of Starbucks, empty but for the foamy dregs, a crumpled greasy bag from Greggs that held my cheese-and-tomato croissant, the cheap blue biro that ran dry after only a sentence. I write them in, I make myself write them in, to anchor myself. To tell a story is to travel between worlds, to open up portals between past and present, and I mustn't get lost there: get distracted by phantoms and lose the way back. Portals between worlds: it seems an over-the-top way of putting it, but that's what it's felt like these past few weeks, as I've been plagued by memories. I've started – I've opened the gates – and so I'll have to finish. I'm going to go back to my flat, now, and sit down with my laptop and plunge straight into the second part of the holiday in Fuengirola, and I'm not going to stop until it's all told, done.

The aqua park

It was the fifth day of our week-long holiday. The days had passed, longer and slower than holiday days should, because we were in such a state of suspension; waiting; worry. We made friends with some of the other children and roamed around the complex with them, playing games and causing low-level havoc. We desperately wanted to go to the beach, which was only a short bus ride away, but didn't dare, for fear of missing our father if he phoned, or arrived. So we hung around the complex, and our days took on a routine. There was a little shop on site selling blow-up lilos, suntan lotion, ice creams and soft drinks, day-old *Daily Mail*s that I flipped through for news of Northern Ireland, and bread and croissants each morning. Alfie and I would go down each day to buy breakfast and we'd all eat together, then the two of us would get changed into our costumes and our mother would rub us with sun cream and we'd splash about in the pool until the midday sun grew too strong. Lunch was sandwiches or omelette and chips from the bar; afternoons spent back in the pool. In the evening there were kids' discos and karaoke, themed entertainment nights. Our mother joined in with none of it. She lay on a lounger on the patch of coarse grass in front of our apartment and sunbathed there, sometimes reading her book, sometimes just lying. She rarely spoke to us, even at mealtimes. We spent as little time near her as possible, I'm ashamed to admit. I think we were scared of her, then, the big brown circles under her eyes; the way she'd crumble her croissant with her fingers into piles of greasy flakes.

And still no Dad.

Every morning at nine o'clock our mother spoke to our father, and every day he said he was hopeful of coming the following day. It was coming up to the Twelfth of July in Ireland, marching season. People rioted, threw stones and broken bottles and petrol bombs; doctors in hospitals, and surgeons in particular, were needed on standby. There was a television in the club house and Alfie and I sneaked in often to watch the news and see if things were really as bad as we feared, but it showed nothing but football and Spanish game shows on a loop. On the third morning I went with my mother to the phone in reception and she passed over the receiver and I begged my father to come in time for my birthday. His voice cracked on the other end of the telephone and he promised, he promised he'd try. I was desperate to ask him how bad things really were there, but my mother was hovering right behind me, ready to take back the phone, and so I didn't dare. She hated, loathed, all talk of the 'Troubles' as it was so grotesquely, euphemistically called. If you didn't know the place except through the news it was impossible to believe that people actually lived there – went about their daily routines of making their sandwiches for lunch and rinsing out their cereal bowls and mopping the floors and going for haircuts and checking the weather forecast for the weekend. I often used to think about

that. Children lived there – children like me and Alfie
– going to school, not wanting to go to school. Slinging
their uniforms on the floor when they came home and
being shouted at to pick them up. Eating jam on toast and
watching *SuperTed* and *Bananaman*. Pound Puppies and
Transformers and Cabbage Patch Kids: they had them,
too. The sounds of their parents watching *Blind Date*.
Growing cress eggmen on the windowsill. All you ever
saw on the news were snarling dogs and faceless policemen in riot gear, the blackened, mangled remains of a bus
or shop or a car, the balaclavas and guns, the loose-faced,
glazed-eyed families of the victims. But behind it was a
whole layer of other lives, lives like ours. We mentioned
none of it in our house, ever, and so I thought about it for
days on end, sometimes.

I passed the phone slowly back to my mother and
she took it in both hands like something precious and
pressed it to her ear, then flapped her hand at me to shoo
me away. Before I was out of earshot I could hear her
voice cracking, just as my dad's had, just as I knew mine
had, as she too begged him to come for my birthday.

We'd finished breakfast and were getting ready to go to
the pool. It must have been half past eight or so, quarter
to nine – not yet time for the daily phone call. Our mother had sun-creamed Alfie and now it was my turn: I was
standing in my pink and yellow bikini, holding my strag-
gly ponytail out of the way with one hand and gripping
the top of the sofa with the other, trying not to hop about
at each cold gloop of cream. Our apartment, as I've said,
was on the ground floor. Its doors opened right out onto

a little terracotta patio and the lawn. Alfie was squatting down watching a lizard in the bougainvillea by the low stone wall and suddenly he leapt to his feet and froze for a moment, then hurled himself forward out of sight. I twisted round to see what was happening and my mother told me to keep still and at the same time Alfie started shouting, Daddy, Daddy, *Daddy*! For a moment, my mother and I looked at each other. But this time was different: before I knew it, I was hurtling out of the flat, too, still slick with sun cream, the coarse grass and stony path below my bare feet immaterial, and *there he was*. Alfie was already clinging to him, legs wrapped around his waist, and I flung myself at him, too, and we were all three of us tangled up and breathless with laughter. I was so excited, so relieved to finally see him that I didn't notice when our mother came around the corner, or that she'd stopped a little distance off and was just standing there in her kimono, messy-haired and un-made-up.

'Patrick,' she said, and then again, 'Patrick?'

We stopped our crowing and our hooting and Dad prised Alfie's legs loose and slid him down to the ground. Then he cleared his throat and took a step forwards.

'Hello, Jane,' he said.

A moment later, they too were in each other's arms. Our father was a huge bear of a man, well over six feet tall and broad with it, and our mother was a little bird of a creature. He swamped her – engulfed her – lifted her off her feet with the force of his embrace. Then Alfie and I rushed back to them, too, sucked in by their force field. We must have looked like such a happy family.

The embrace loosened. We made our way back to the apartment, Alfie and I chattering at Dad about the swimming pool and the lizards and had he noticed how brown we were, tugging down the edges of our costumes to show our tan lines. Inside, we swooped with glee on the canvas holdall he'd been carrying, bore it ceremoniously to the kitchen table and almost broke the zip in our haste to get inside. Our father always brought us presents when he came back from Ireland. He had brought us a pair of tacky toy donkeys wearing sombreros and two fluorescent T-shirts – one pink, one green – with *Welcome to Marbella!* printed on them. For our mother, there was a bottle of almond liqueur wrapped in straw, fake peasant-style. They were the sort of things we'd seen in the complex's gift shop, the sort of things you could buy in any of the eight, ten shops lining the road opposite. They were the sort of things we'd coveted on our first day and our mother had said weren't worth wasting money on. We tried not to show our disappointment but our father sensed it. The presents hadn't even been wrapped. When we tried them on, the pink T-shirt was tight on me, while Alfie's green one swamped him.

'There were all I could manage,' he said, glancing at our mother.

She said nothing.

'Here, wee love,' he said, turning to me. 'I'll say this now and I'll say it right away. I've not got your birthday present with me. It'll have to wait – OK? Until we're back at home.'

I nodded, and smiled.

'It's just nice to see you, Daddy,' I said. I meant it: and I thought saying it would make things better, but instead it caused an odd and sudden silence.

Our father was the one who rallied. 'Well now,' he said. 'What are we going to do today, eh? I thought – how's this for a plan, yousens? – that we'd go to . . .' – he paused for effect – 'an aqua park. How's about it?'

With that, of course, everything else was forgotten and we capered at him, jumping up and down and squealing.

'There's one just up the coast,' he said to our mother. She said something back but I heard no more of the conversation because Alfie and I were rushing into our bedrooms to get our T-shirts and shorts and sandals and goggles.

When we came out, our parents were kissing and our mother was crying.

'Are you crying, Mum? Why are you crying?' Alfie said.

'I'm not crying,' she said, but she was: our father had been holding her face in his hands and flicking away the tears with his thumbs, as you might do with a child.

'Come on, Mum,' I said – cruelly, it seems now, but I think it came from a sudden lurch of the same fear I'd felt on the plane, or when she made me promise never to say to Dad we'd been to Ireland. 'You're the only one we're waiting for. You're holding things up.'

The aqua park was the most exciting place we'd ever seen. The high blue tubes of the coiled covered flumes were visible from half a mile away, and as we drove into the car park you could hear the shrieks and the music and smell the bleached tang of the chlorine.

My memory slows at this point. I want to remember these moments and hold every one of them, hold us, in my mind's eye, for as long as possible. Cast my net of words around us and draw it tight. The cool, dank changing rooms and the slimy feel of the concrete underneath. Bundling my clothes into Mum's and my locker, jumping from foot to foot as she unbuckled each of her sandals and folded her kaftan, unnecessarily methodical, unnecessarily precise. Slamming the tinny door and wriggling out the key on its thick, faded elastic band. The greenish footbaths, warm and viscous as saliva, and the lukewarm spray of the obligatory showers. Dad and Alfie already waiting, the hairy animal man and the birdlike boy – a sudden jolt of shyness, because my father was so male, the tight coils of black hair on his chest, oiled down but springing loose, and the whorls of hair on his upper arms and back. I'd never seen him, could not remember seeing him, so fleshy, so naked. A gust of breeze made me shiver and I hugged my towel across my tight, not-quite-budding breasts, suddenly shy, self-conscious. Dad reached for Mum's hand and we made our way, the four of us, along the rough red path and down to the snack bar area, where palm trees and rattan umbrellas gave some shade, past the shallow kiddie pool where man-sized penguins and elephants spouted water from their trunks and beaks, to where white-bright loungers lay in rows. We staked our spot, dragging four loungers together, and laid out our beach towels. Our parents, it seemed, weren't going to rush to go on the rubber-ring rides and log flumes. They wanted to have a coffee, sunbathe, talk. Alfie and I were torn, then, between wanting to be with them – to be with our father – and the call of the rides. Alfie was too small for some of the rides and others had warnings up saying that under-twelves had to be accompanied by an adult. But we could go on the slides and in the pool with the wave machine. Our mother, I could tell, was impatient for us to go. She ushered us on, told us to stay together, for me to look after Alfie; promised that if we came back in an hour, she and our father would take us on the adult rides – the ones with names like 'Black Hole' and 'Kamikaze'.

We ran off, then. I remember how blue the day was: the sky was blue, the slides were blue and the water was the bluest blue I'd ever seen. It was still only morning – about eleven o'clock, perhaps, or half past ten – but the sun was beating down in waves, you could almost see it, and the rough ground was warm underfoot. There was a queue to get to the water slides, but it moved fast enough. The attendants, bored under their baseball caps, limbs burnished by the sun, were practised at dispatching yelping children. There were four slides, all joined together, and Alfie and I went in the two middle ones. I can see us there, now, clutching on to the thin metal pole, tugged forwards by the sluice of water, waiting for the go-ahead. I can almost feel it: the lurch of the first, plummeting drop, then skidding and bumping sideways and down to land in a plume of foam. We come up shouting and spluttering, hair sleeked to our heads, with slow swimmy echoes in our ears where the water has run in. The attendant is calling out for us to clear the way, and we doggy-paddle to the edge and clamber out, shaking our heads and gulping to clear our ears, and I wring the water from my long thin rope of a ponytail, then we seize hands and run back up, again, again.

The hour passes, and more, before we've realised. The aqua park is busier now, the queues longer, the music turned up louder. We race back down to our parents. You almost have to race, now, taking your feet off the ground as soon as they touch it: it's baking under the midday sun. Our parents are sitting up, watching for us, making hand-visors and peering up into the sun. Dad has his other hand on Mum's neck and he's clasping it, squeezing it. He has beautiful fingers – long, tapered, delicate – which look incongruous, as if they've been grafted onto the bulk of him. They are the sort of fingers pianists have, or artists. I know: I've got them too. I got my father's bulk, as well – his 'big bones', as people consolingly said once I became a teenager – though with our mother's height, the worst possible combination. But there'll be time for that later. For now, we're running about, gabbling about the water slides, the splashes . . . And we're suddenly starving – the smells of hot dogs and frying onions, the buttery smell of popcorn, are coming from the snack area, and we want hot dogs and rustling, salty chips in paper cups – but our mother says we won't be able to swim for an hour after we've eaten, so we decide to go on one ring-ride first. We each take one of Dad's hands as we lead him towards the one we've chosen – 'Black Hole' – and I feel a momentary pang for Mum, following behind us, but she must understand that it's just we always see her, every day. At the entrance to the queue, the attendant is making all children stand beside a metal stick to see if they're tall enough. Alfie ruffs up his hair, like in his *Tintin* books, and hovers on the balls of his feet, but he's still too small. So he has to stay at the bottom with Mum, who says she's not that keen anyway, and it's Dad and I who go through, and I have him all to myself.

We climb the steps, right to the top, holding our clumsy, chlorine-beaded rubber tyres – mine almost as big as me – and join the shuffling queue.

'All right, wee Squrl?' Dad says. 'Monkey-boy' is Dad's nickname for Alfie and I'm 'Squirrel', or 'Squrl', as he pronounces it, the relic of some long-forgotten babyhood joke.

I beam at him. 'I knew you'd come in time for my birthday,' I blurt out. 'I knew it.'

He looks at me, then nods. 'Come you here, Squrl.' He grips me to him, and I nestle in against his solid, warm side.

The coiled tubes of the 'Black Hole' reach much higher than the water slides. From the top, through the railings, we can see the scrublands to the north, littered with palm trees and the concrete bones of new developments; and past the glinting heat of the car park, the glittering sea to the south. There is a breeze up here, and the sound of crickets is louder than the Europop coming from the speakers down below. We've left it all behind. We are kings of the world, up here.

'Africa's that way,' Dad says. 'If you kept going long enough in that direction, you'd hit Morocco.'

'And Ireland?'

'Ah, Ireland. Ireland's a long way behind us, now. Almost the opposite direction.'

A group of giggling teenage girls is immediately ahead of us. I am shy of them – shy of their filled-out bikini tops and rounded bottoms. They are talking in loud, fast Spanish and one of them says something and they look at my dad and me and laugh. I slip my hand out of his and I think I've done it casually but he glances down at me and then at the teenagers.

'This is going to be your last year,' he says. 'Before you're a terrible teenager, I mean.' He sounds sad, suddenly: very far away.

I want to say something but I don't know what. Neither of us says anything more for a while.

The girls are dispatched, shrieking, and now it is our turn.

'Do you want to go first, or do you want me to go first?'

'You go first, Dad.'

So he does, clambering with all the awkwardness of his bulk into the bright yellow tyre and letting the gum-chewing attendant shove him spinning into the mouth of the tube. The yell he gives out resounds and hangs in the air for seconds after he's gone and I am suddenly scared and I don't want to follow him down there. But there's no time to change my mind: suddenly it is me climbing into the holding pool and the thigh-deep attendant steadying my ring as I haul myself onto it, and gripping the handles for dear life I am sent hurling into the dank rushing darkness. In those few, suspended seconds it takes to hurtle round and round the tube, bumping sideways and turning backwards, the only thought in my mind is that my father's done it too and he's at the bottom waiting for me.

After lunch, despite ourselves, we are glad to rest for a while, warm and lazy on our loungers in the sun. Mum pushes her and Dad's loungers together and lowers the arms, so they're almost one, and they lie there, she in the crook of his arm, pulled in to his chest. In almost all my memories of them together, I realise, they are this close. Touching, kissing, leaning on each other. Even as they ate, he'd have a hand on her knee; as they walked along, they'd be holding hands, or his palm would be in the small of her back. She was forever stroking his face, twisting her hands in his hair, he bending to kiss her forehead or shoulders, wherever she had skin exposed. You'd think, if you watched them, that nothing could ever come between them. They looked, and I'm sure it's not just in my mind's eye, like the very picture of a couple deeply in love.

Later on, we swim in the pool with the wave machine, which is turned on every hour on the hour, and Alfie and I have a few more goes on the water slides. The sun, though still fiercely bright, is lower in the sky now. People are starting to pack up and go and we know our parents are going to say it's home-time soon. I suddenly want one more go on one of the bigger rides – the 'Kamikaze' this time – and I decide I want to do it on my own, and see my father's face when I tell him. So I make Alfie wait by the fence and I go up again, by myself. Near the top, I turn to wave at Alfie, and he waves back, and I wonder if I can see my parents from here. I find the snack area, and the loungers, and count my way along until I can see their shapes, and our towels. My mother's body, despite her four-days tan, looks pale and very small beside my father's: and something strikes me that hasn't occurred to me before. How tanned he is. All over his body, back and front, his skin is the red-brown of someone who's been in the sun. It's been raining in Belfast, I know, I've seen the photos in the *Daily Mail* and followed the weather forecasts, desperate for any news from there. All week, a thick, dreary rain and low, dull skies. Why would my father be tanned, and why haven't I noticed it until now?

The skin pimples on my arms and legs, although there is no breeze, and a boy behind me nudges me to move forward and close the gap that's opened up in the queue. I bump the rubber tyre along with my foot but I don't want to do this any more. Something isn't quite right: the feelings I've had, since the afternoon my mother was so inexplicably angry and upset about Ireland, since the gin-and-tonics and sunglasses on the plane and the horrible wait in the terminal building, her crying this morning, the glimpse of golf clubs I had in the boot of Dad's car, it all surges back and I have a bitter, dry taste at the back of my mouth and throat, as if I might vomit.

The ride is no fun this time. I judder and swoosh to the bottom then wriggle out of the tyre and drag it from the deep end to the shallow, and out. Alfie is cheering me and I snap at him to shut up and he looks at me, big-eyed and startled.

'Come on, stupid.'

We make our way back to the loungers, this churning feeling inside of me. Our parents are sitting waiting for us, their towels rolled up, ready to go. Mum holds out my towel for me and when I'm close enough for her to see my face she puts it down and reaches out her arm instead.

'What's wrong?'

My father steps forward, tilts up my chin so he can see my face. 'C'mere, pet. What's happened?'

'She came off the ride and yelled at me,' Alfie starts.

'Shut up, Alfie.'

'Don't talk to your brother like that. What's happened, Lara? Did you hurt yourself?'

I look at my mother, and from her to my father. All the things I want to say are swilling in my stomach. Does he have cancer? That's one of them. I know that you have to have radiation when you have cancer, and maybe that gives you a tan. Another is: are they getting divorced? Another is: does he want us to move to Ireland, or does he want to go to America, or somewhere, and we're going to have to leave London, and our flat, and our friends? None of these things are right and I know it. I stare at my father and can't find the words for any of it.

'It was the ride,' I say. 'I think I swallowed too much water.'

'My poor wee Squrl,' Dad says, and goes to hug me. I take a step away from him and he looks hurt. Part of me feels mean for hurting him, but part of me is glad in a way that I don't understand.

We're walking back from the changing rooms to the car park when Alfie says, 'Can we come back here tomorrow? Please can we? For Lara's birthday?' and there is a silence. My mother actually stops walking.

'Come on, love,' Dad murmurs. 'Not here.'

'No, Alfie,' she says, and her voice is tight and high. 'No, we can't come back tomorrow.'

'Why not? Oh please . . ?'

'Come on, Monkey-boy. Don't spoil a perfect day. It's been a perfect day, hasn't it, Lara? Apart from you swallowing half the pool, eh? Here, why don't you spit it back before we leave, I don't want them charging me extra,' our father says in his easy, joking way. He catches Alfie round the waist and swings him up onto his shoulders, with a grunt – Alfie is just about small enough for him to do this.

Our father is an expert at changing the subject.

We get back to the complex and Dad comes and takes another shower, even though we showered at the aqua park. Then he puts on his clothes – and why is he wearing, I suddenly wonder, two-tone golfing shoes and ankle socks, shorts and a polo shirt and even a visor?

You don't need to see our incomprehension, and anger, and our mother's tears. She knew this was a bad idea, she says, they're too old, you can't lie to them. It doesn't come out quite so neatly as this but I'll spare you the tears, the scenes where our father peels us off him and pleads with us, with me, to forgive him for missing my birthday tomorrow. I'll spare you the sight of our mother, silent as a statue, as if she's disappeared and shrunken somewhere into the depths of herself. The sight of the car, a maroon saloon, pulling away and not stopping, and Alfie running after it, and me yanking him back, and then despite myself running after it myself. Both of us crying, sobbing our little hearts out – a dark-eyed man from one of the tourist shops coming over to offer us (you wouldn't make this up) one of those damn donkeys our father had tried to fob us off with. I want to hurl it at him, to scream – but I'm too well-mannered for that. Instead, I take it, say a stiff thank-you, then grab Alfie's hand and drag him back inside our compound, and back to our apartment, where our mother is standing exactly as we left her.

My father, you see, as I'm just beginning to guess, is living a lie. The lie is us. Our father has another wife – or rather, I should say, a wife, because it turns out that he and my mother aren't, as I have always assumed, actually married at all. He lives with her in Belfast, the real wife, with her and their children – his other children, his real children. They are up the coast, in a hotel in Marbella, and they know nothing about us, at all. As far as they're concerned, their husband, their father, is returning home after a long day's golfing, ready to have a cocktail at the hotel bar, then dinner in a fancy restaurant. My father's wife is called Catriona Connolly. Their daughter, who is a year and a half older than me, is Veronica Louise. Their son is Patrick Michael, known as Michael.

I realise I haven't named my father yet, not properly. I'll name him here with them, where he most belongs. That sentence, even after all these years, is difficult to write, but it's true. His name was Patrick Michael Connolly. We don't have his name, Alfie and I. He's not named on either of our birth certificates. We, like our mother, are Moorhouses.

Of course it doesn't come out as neatly as this. I'm starting to get into what I pieced together in the weeks and months afterwards, the tangled web of lies and logistics. What my mother tells us that evening is that it's like our father is divorced, except he can't leave his first family. But she's a terrible liar, my mother. We can tell by her silent tears, rolling down a face as stricken as ours, that she's not telling the whole story.

Sunday evening blues

The best thing about the Monday writing classes is the shape and purpose they give to Sunday evenings. The long, flabby hours; the washed-out, grey despair that sets in around three o'clock and stretches until nine, or half past nine, or ten, or whatever hour you can persuade yourself is a reasonable time to take a Zimovane and go to bed.

Sundays in my childhood were the day when our father would have left, and there'd be two weeks to go before he was back. In your teens and twenties you can go out and get trashed on a Sunday night with other people who feel the same. In a couple, you can sink the day into long lunches that stretch boozy into the evening, or pub quizzes, or even if you do nothing but takeaway and telly there's both of you, there's company. On your own, there is nothing. The world, at the weekend, is full of new couples, shagged-out and mooning at each other. It's full of young parents with babies; families; groups of married friends. Alone in the day on a Saturday, you can be independent, full-of-purpose, getting things done. On a Sunday, there's no way of disguising, even to yourself – especially to yourself – how utterly alone you are. These days, if I'm not on the rota and I don't make plans in advance, the whole day can pass without my speaking to anyone, unless you count a visit to the Costcutter to buy something I don't need for the relief of a human exchange. For a while I went to Alfie's on a Sunday, but I could see they only had me over out of pity. Loneliness is infectious – you trail its miasma around with you – and people sense it unconsciously and want to be away from you. The girls would be fidgety and bored at having to sit in the living room and talk to me; once, I even heard Danielle promising them Bratz dolls if they stayed with their aunt until teatime. A few times we went on excursions. To the garden centre, to a family-friendly pub, to the London Butterfly House at Kew. That was my suggestion – the horror at being the aunt who forces you to trail around a garden centre; I don't even have a window box – and it was the last. The Butterfly House was hugely, steamingly humid – tropical, of course – and the damp flapping butterflies, some the size of dinner plates, nosing their proboscises at blackened banana sludge made the girls run squealing. Afterwards in the café, when I was coming back from the loos, I heard them complaining about having to do boring things with their aunt on Sundays, and I decided not to trouble the family again. It isn't their fault. They're only little. Their Sundays should be spent doing things they want to do: going skating or swimming, or adventure playgrounds. So Mr Rawalpindi's writing classes were a lifeline, because now I reserve Sundays to do the exercises, even if I don't hand them in, and to think over the issues the tutor has asked us to ponder for the following night, even if I don't participate in class.

Tomorrow we're looking at how to introduce characters and establish their world. The teacher touched on this at the end of last week's session. A mistake that new writers often make, she said, is to take you through who all the characters are in a schoolmistressy way, before the story even begins. Shoehorning in biographies and backstories which clog up the narrative and stop the story from gathering pace. We are going to learn how to avoid this. But I've been thinking about it all day and I've come to the conclusion that although that might be fine in fiction, when you're making up a world and are completely in charge of the cast of characters – how many of them there are, how and when they appear, and everything else – it doesn't quite work with my story. Already, scrolling through the pages I've written, I see so many names it must be bewildering. My father and mother, me and Alfie, Catriona, Veronica, Michael. Jeremy and Mr Rawalpindi, the writing tutor. Danielle and Alfie's girls. Not to mention the cameo roles, the characters who appear briefly once or twice. This is, above all, my father and mother's story, so I'll take pains to describe them as fully as I can. Alfie too, and Danielle and their girls. The next chapter I write, I've decided, will be about the other family, and the time we went to Belfast to confront them. And I feel I should describe Mr Rawalpindi and Jeremy, and of course the writing teacher, people who aren't really part of this story but who are hovering at its edges. I want you to see them, as well, or at least know who they are.

I wonder, too, if I should describe myself. I don't know how much of a sense you can get of someone just by reading their words. In some ways you know me far better than if you'd just met me, because you have access to my most intimate thoughts: but in other ways, you know me far less. You don't know what I look like. On the list of things we were to think about before tomorrow, the teacher has written: Is a character's physical appearance strictly relevant to the story? In terms of this story, I suppose the answer is no. I'm not writing a romcom or a chick lit or the sort of book where a hero is going to appear and see through my physical appearance to the true me. If I was writing that, I would describe me, because it would be important that I'm not exactly a catch. As it is, the story isn't even really about me at all: it's about my childhood, and my parents. So what I look like, and what job I do, and the rest of it, shouldn't matter at all. Personally, though, I like to picture my narrator in my head while I read, so perhaps a brief description of me would help.

Here goes. As I said at the start, I'm on the wrong side of my thirties. Thirty-nine in a few weeks' time. Which is not a good age to be when you're newly single, not of your own volition, and with no immediate prospects – to be blunt about it. I have my mother's height – short – and my father's build: sturdy. My hair is sort of nondescript, and I dye it, these days to cover the grey. When I was a teenager it was pink, blue, striped with green. Purple, once, to match my DM boots. Nowadays it's 'plum', 'burgundy', 'chocolate', 'rich chestnut', deep, comforting names that inevitably look nothing like they sound, or like the packet. At the moment, my hair is a sort of dull reddish-brown, cut above my shoulders in a nothingy style that's an attempt to grow out my immediately post-Jeremy bob. My eyes, grey; my face, pale, sort of oval.

I work as an Agency Carer, which means that I go around giving non-medical assistance to a changing rota of clients. Usually, they're old people who aren't yet old or ill enough to need a residential home or full-time care. They might have had a stroke, or a knee or back injury, or some other incapacitating illness, and need help going up or down stairs, getting washed or dressed, or eating their meals. They might have the onset of dementia, or Alzheimer's, or some form of senility or other mental illness. I can change their dressings, check they've taken the right combinations of medicines at the right times. Sponge-bath them, or help them in and out of their bath, or wash and dry their hair, or help them apply their makeup. Cook for them, occasionally, or cut up their meat into bite-sized pieces, or wield a spoon for them. A lot of my job involves listening to them: what most people want above all is a bit of company and a chat, and after you've done the physical things required they force cups of tea and slices of stale Battenberg or crumbling custard creams on you. Sometimes you see a person every day for a fortnight, then never again. Sometimes it's twice a week for a year or more: until their condition deteriorates, or they die, or their family moves them elsewhere. I get my rota for the week every Monday from the agency – usually I phone in, and they email it across. Sometimes two of you are needed – if there's a lot of lifting work involved, or the client is obese, or has a tendency to violence – or occasionally I'll be asked to take a trainee along with me. On the whole, though, it's a solitary job.

This seems like the right moment to introduce Mr Rawalpindi. Although I call him by his first name to his face, these days, it seems a courtesy to keep him as 'Mr Rawalpindi' here. One thing that people often don't realise is that elderly or sick people don't like being called by their first names. They find it infantilising: demeaning. I always make a point of calling my patients by their surname, until they specifically ask me otherwise. Mr Rawalpindi I've known for more than two years, now – he's one of my longest-standing clients. There's no time or space for favourites in my job. You can see up to ten, twelve clients a day, some days, although the norm is more like five or six; and most of the time the half-hour or hour allotted isn't enough to do what's necessary. Sometimes, it's as little as fifteen minutes, which is nothing, except that the alternative is unthinkable. It's strictly discouraged by the agency to grow friendly with people or to overstay the allotted time. If someone seems terribly lonely, though, or if you grow to know someone, it's hard not to use up your breaks or your lunchtime sitting with them. It was like that with Mr Rawalpindi, at first. He lives alone in a huge, rambling, filthy old house in Hammersmith, not too far from me. He's got osteoarthritis, and he's had both prostate and colorectal cancer, and wears a colostomy bag – his body is quite literally disintegrating around him. His mind, though, is sharp and sly and bright and witty as anything, and some days I think it's by sheer force of will that he holds himself together. He vows that he's never going into a care home: he'll die rather than that. Never, he says, were there two more baldly euphemistic words yoked together. He lives in a downstairs room of his house, as he finds stairs difficult. Some days I go upstairs in search of some box of photographs or mementoes; other days I just do a little cooking for him, or tidy up. These days I call in out of hours, on my way to or from work; bring him shopping; sit and talk with him. He's full of the most outrageous stories – his childhood in the West Indies, his homosexual conquests, how he ended up with his massive ramshackle house – and at the start of the year he began to be obsessed with writing his memoirs. Every time I went round he'd want more damp boxes exhumed and he'd have more yellowed file paper covered in headings and possible chapter titles and scribblings. It was he who found out about the Introductory Classes to Creative Writing at the Irish Cultural Centre and blagged himself a place, although he's got nothing whatsoever to do with Ireland. He persuaded me to come along with him and now every Monday evening we make our way there, odd pair that we are, him dangerous-driving along the pavement on his souped-up mobility scooter – West Indies Federation flag, hand-painted rainbow – and me trotting behind carrying his walking sticks and yelling at him to slow down and watch out.

The writing teacher is Irish, naturally, very young and enthusiastic. She talks in sentences that could come straight out of a novel themselves, and she believes, or so she keeps telling us, that fiction can change the world. Mr Rawalpindi, I think, is a little in love with her. He recognises a kindred, Pollyanna spirit. The rest of us oddballs just blush or stare at our feet when she asks us a question.

So that just leaves Jeremy. I've been putting him off. I'd really rather not write about him at all, but I suppose I have to, so I'll get him out of the way as quickly and briefly as possible. Jeremy was – is – a geography teacher at a sixth-form college and we were together for almost seven years. We lived together – in his flat – for four of those years and I think I supposed we'd be together for the long haul. He was never keen on marriage, but that was fine, because – no surprises – neither was I. He was also ambivalent about children, and one of his pet riffs was that the world was overpopulated as it was, and a child was worth an Eiffel Tower of carbon dioxide. That was fine, too. I wasn't desperately broody, and we slotted in, or ticked along together, or whatever the right phrase might be. Something easy, indeterminate. We'd accumulated mutual friends, habits, everything that life with someone else accrues. I don't claim we were madly in love, but then, I don't think that most people are. Nastasya and Aleksander, my father and mother, they're the exception. For most people, I imagine it's something like Jeremy and me: you meet when you've turned thirty (he was thirty-six) and you're ready to settle down. My first – my only – serious boyfriend before Jeremy was when I was sixteen. He was the conclusive act of rebellion in my teenage years. He was fifteen years older, unemployed, already divorced. You don't have to be a psychologist to work it out. At first I thought he was a true gentleman. It was only later I realised how controlling he was, and how sex for him wasn't something fun, something you did for love or even lust, like with the other boys my age: for him it was the ultimate power play. Some days he would yank my hair and forbid me to look him in the eye. Other times he would insist on pleasuring me first, keeping the palm of his hand on the part of my belly just above my pelvis, to make sure I was coming and not faking. When I left him, he said I was frigid and I'd never find another man. He knew how much I was scared of that. He knew me well enough that he could make a grenade, just like that, and chuck it casually over his shoulder at me. He took up five years of my life, and was a large part of the reason I never made it to university. I was pretty messed up after that, for most of my twenties, and with Jeremy I thought I'd found peace, or at least security; normality and routine. The sex was never great but it was fine. We sometimes argued, but mostly we rubbed along, and there were times we had a lot of fun. Then out of the blue one evening, last summer, he announced it wasn't working and we should break up. I don't want to go into the bewilderment and humiliation of that. Six months after my mother had died, too, and I was still dealing with the fallout from that: the sorting of her things, the selling of her house. And somehow, within a fortnight, I was having to move out of my home and into this scuzzy basement flat that I couldn't have afforded without Alfie's help and the little money my mother left me. Without that, I'd have been on Gumtree or worse, looking for lodgings in some stranger's flat. (Mr Rawalpindi, bless him, offered me the use of a room in his house, and it's a mark of how desperate I was that I almost accepted it, unethical as it would have been.) At Christmas, I heard through mutual friends that Jeremy had a new girlfriend, and by New Year she wasn't just his girlfriend but his fiancée and they were pregnant. I stalked them on Facebook for a while – he'd unfriended me, but I got to their pictures through other people –

until I decided it was unhealthy and deactivated my account.

The baby will be due any time now: has maybe already been born.

There is one more character in this story, an invisible one, that hovers between the lines of everything I write. It's the spectre of the children I know I won't have, now. I'm writing about my own parents, and how they fucked up, but I'm writing about myself, too, mourning the loss of something I won't now have. It was a strange and terrible sensation learning that Jeremy had found someone so quickly, that a man who's always been against marriage and children can decide at the age of forty-five that that's what he does want, after all. A woman doesn't have that luxury. Into the vacuum that he left came rushing all kinds of urges that I didn't even know I had, things I'd suppressed, or hadn't had, or hadn't allowed myself to have. You do read the odd story of a woman who gave birth at forty-three, forty-five, forty-eight, without IVF or the rest of it, and to a healthy child. Mostly, though, the media is full of women who leave it too late for a baby, women who can't have a baby, the ticking time bomb of infertility inside of us that's ready to go off – boom! – and turn your womb into a scorched, dry, arid place where nothing can ever grow again. Every glossy magazine you read is full of warnings that your fertility declines so severely in your thirties that it's half what it was even by the time you've finished reading this article. But there's little I can do about it, I want to scream back. There's nobody on the scene, and I'm not likely to meet one in my job, or any time soon. My flat's not suitable for a baby – it's barely big enough for one person, and even cats are prohibited. I couldn't afford it, not the baby itself nor the time not working. Yet I can't stop the yearning. Sometimes it feels like a tugging, an actual tugging, deep in my pelvis and womb. It's not entirely rational, what I'm feeling, and I know it's not just to do with Jeremy: it's to do with losing my own mother, too, and both events happening so close together. It's a sort of mourning for myself, and for my life, for mothers and motherhood. But I can't seem to stop it, or assuage it, and it keeps me awake at night.

Before I started writing this, I'd taken to searching databases of sperm donors, wondering if I could or should do it myself, even though the only possible answer was: No. There have been problems with the sale of my mother's house – possible asbestos, and some subsidence – but once it's sold I'll have some money, and perhaps this will be what I'll do with it. The Danish clinics, all websites tell you, are the best. For free, and even without signing up, you can scroll through donors organised by race, ethnicity, hair and eye colour, height, weight, blood type, education, occupation, almost any criterion you can think of. You can see photos of them – most have pictures of themselves as babies and toddlers, of course, because that's what you'll be getting. Some even have audio interviews, so you can hear their voices, talking perfect, clipped Scandinavian English for twenty- or thirty-second bursts. All of them have short profiles, written by staff at the clinic. *Aake is a very creative and organised person. He is a perfectionist when it comes to his education and he sets*

73

himself very high goals in this matter. He has just gotten his Diploma as a Graphic Designer and is now looking for a job to launch his career. Thick brown hair and blue eyes characterise Aake. His eyes are ones you can easily get lost in. The skin tone is fair but he can get a great tan in the summertime, without getting burned. He is in great physical shape . . . And so forth. Below will be a list of Aake's 'stock' of donations. Each is graded: if it is 'IUI-ready', 'ICI-unwashed'; the quality in terms of density and motility. There are lists of prices – MOT5, say, costs 74 euros for 0.4 ml whereas MOT40 costs 370 euros – and instructions on how and when to place an order, how to store an order, how to tell when you're at your most fertile, how to self-inseminate if you don't have the means to travel to the clinic in Denmark. They make it sound so rational, so reasonable, so possible.

I probably sound crazy. I sound like every magazine's worst stereotype of a single woman nearing forty: lonely, desperate, probably unhinged. I don't even know if I'd actually do it: it's just the knowing that there's a way out, that there's something I can *do*. Feeling, more and more each day that the escape routes out of your current life are rapidly closing down around you.

It's suddenly gone eleven: the writing of this has managed to kill the whole of a hated Sunday evening. That's no small mercy, and for that alone I won't delete this yet, though the shame at what I've written is starting to curdle in my stomach. I've gone way off course with this. None of it I meant to say. Last Monday we were talking about the importance of planning, the dangers of

launching into something and going off track and getting lost in the wilderness. I've managed to ignore all of
it. But the thing is: this isn't some neat, plotted, made-up
story. I don't have that luxury.

The other family

The time we went to visit the other family, my mother and I, was of course the secret trip to Belfast, the forbidden one, the one she didn't think I remembered. After the revelations of Fuengirola, it suddenly made some sense. To my intense frustration, however, the hours spent dredging my memory have yielded only a few results; a handful of grit. The little that I do know, or have surmised or pieced together, is as follows.

It was while she was pregnant with Alfie – I remember her big, taut tummy, the way I put my ear to it and used to listen for the baby – so it must have been 1977. I know I entered a Reception class the autumn Alfie was born, and I don't think that had started yet, so it must have been late August. I would have just turned four, and my mother must have been almost exactly six months pregnant. That was why she went over: to confront Catriona Connolly in person, with her swollen belly and school-age daughter, evidence that her affair with Patrick had been going on for more than five years, now.

Five years – half a decade – it's almost unimaginable. Five years and two children, and she still hasn't left him, or made him tell his wife. I wonder now why she didn't telephone. Choose a time when she knew my father was at the hospital, or mid-air. Perhaps that wasn't enough: a

76

phone call could be dismissed more easily than a pregnant woman standing there, than a little girl unmistakably her daddy's daughter. My mother was upping the stakes, double or quits, forcing a resolution to a situation which must have been getting untenable.

What I remember most about the trip is the overnight ferry – it would have been from Heysham to Belfast. It's the only time in my childhood we took an overnight ferry and so I know my memories of it are true, that they belong to this trip. If I concentrate, I can at least dredge some of them up. It was still light when we arrived – by coach from Victoria, I suppose – at the ferry terminal. We walked along the harbour, thick with the queasy smell of diesel, and I squatted to look for fish through the railings. We ate pale, flabby chips and limp battered fish in the terminal café, and Mum let me scrape the leftovers into a napkin to throw to the seagulls. It was twilight when we finally boarded the ferry and our cabins weren't ready until an hour after sailing. I dozed on and off in Mum's lap, waking when the juddering engines rolled and turned deep in the bowels of the ship, and we went out on deck to watch the land slide away. All the lights were on – I remember this – and so we stood on the salt-slick deck with the wind tangling our hair and watched them twinkling, smaller and smaller. After a while the wind got stronger, colder, was sore in my ears. I remember that, too. People who'd been out on deck started to go back in. A woman – that's right – was being sick over the railing, and beige spatters flew back on deck. My mother didn't notice. We stood there a long time, as I recall: until we must have been out in the Irish Sea, past the sight of land-lights. The wind by now must have been stronger, blowing in huge buffeting gusts, throwing sprays of sea over us, as wet as if it was raining. I must have gripped the cold, white-painted, blistering railings. Then suddenly, my mother remembers that I'm there and we go back inside. I want to play on the flashing, chirruping one-armed bandits and arcade machines and she won't let me. I start crying, then, and no wonder: it must be very late by now, way past my bedtime, and we've had a long day's travel. Our cabin has a single bed – let's say – and a fold-down bunk. I want the top, but Mum must be worried that I'll fall out, because she makes me sleep in the lower. There is a tiny bathroom, with a toilet and doll-sized sink, and no porthole. That sounds about right, doesn't it?

I'm straining the bounds of my memory, here. I'm writing what could have happened, what probably did. And fiction is no use to me: I need facts, I need the truth. Except that I have no proof: a few flashes – but nothing solid. So what can I say? We take a ferry to Ireland. I sleep. The ferry sails through the night; we wake up in Belfast.

There is a website called CAIN that tells you exactly what was happening in any given year, month, or even day of the Troubles. You just click on the time frame you're interested in and it summarises the main events. Here is what was happening in Northern Ireland that August.

- There was a series of firebomb attacks in Belfast and Lisburn, Co. Antrim.

- The Queen began a two-day visit as part of her Jubilee celebrations. It was her first time in 'the Province' for eleven years.
- The IRA planted a small bomb in the grounds of the new University of Ulster campus. It exploded after the Queen had left and no one was injured.
- Jimmy Carter, then President of the USA, gave a keynote speech on Northern Ireland. In it he called on Americans not to provide financial or other support for groups using violence there.
- This, of course, in addition to a background of general sniper murders (British Army soldiers by the IRA, members of the UDA by the IRA, officers of the RUC by the IRA, members of the Provisional IRA by the Official IRA, and vice versa), beatings, maimings, kneecappings and all the rest of the ugly business that forms a low-level hum to these 'bigger' events.

I've also found out that the mean temperature in Belfast for the last week of August in 1977 – I don't have the date, or any way of finding it out, so that's as good a guess as any – was about 13°C. For the last eight days of the month, it rained, frequently and heavily. There were two days of thunderstorms and pretty bad winds. I wonder what I was wearing, what my mother was wearing. Try as I can to think myself back into that day, I just can't. A rare surviving photo from that winter (a Christmas tree, Alfie a tiny red-faced scrap) shows me in a navy duffel coat with wooden toggles and a red-lined hood, but the fact that I'm wearing it indoors suggests it's new, a Christmas present, perhaps, or a recent purchase I'm proud of. So it

79

can't have been that. Besides, even if Mum had checked the weather forecast, it was August: we wouldn't have worn our winter coats in August, even to Belfast. More likely I am in a thin anorak and Start-rite sandals, a cotton summer dress or pinafore. My mother, six months pregnant, might have been in a Laura Ashley smock, or an empire-line maxi dress. She had a rust-coloured jacket, too, that she'd made herself – she was good at sewing, and made a lot of our clothes from patterns. It had long, flared sleeves and a Nehru collar and it tied under the bust with a yellow ribbon. She loved that coat. Perhaps she wore that – her favourite outfit – or perhaps she dressed smartly for the occasion, bought a sober-coloured jacket and discreet maternity skirt from a department store. What do you wear to meet the wife of your lover – the father of your daughter and unborn child, the man whose flat you've been living in for five years? Do you dress, defiantly, as yourself, or do you try to dress in deference to the occasion? As if you are going to a funeral, say – which in many ways you must feel that you are.

I have had a sudden flash: I seem to remember Mum doing her make-up and fluffing up her hair in the tin-floored cubicle of the toilets at the Belfast terminal. But I could be imagining it; my mind leaping to be helpful, to fill in the gaps in the story. I'm sure she did, though. A touch of blusher to warm up her pale, early-morning, ferry-sick cheeks; a smudge of eyeshadow to accentuate her eyes; the lipstick that she never left the house without, even if we were just going down the road to the library or to Mr Patel's. You don't want to look tarty when you meet your lover's wife, but you want to look confident: self-possessed and groomed. Perhaps she curled her hair, too, in the Velcro rollers she kept in a velvet pouch. Just to add a little volume to her wind-whipped, slept-in hair. Her hair was fine and wavy, lighter brown than mine, and she used to wear it centre-parted and loose, except when she was going to work. If my father was coming, she curled it in heated rollers so that it fell around her shoulders in fat sausages. I'm sure, now that I think about it, that she would have tried to recurl it. Dampening it in the sink with her fingers, winding it up in the rollers and stooping to dry it beneath the hand-dryer.

Did they even have electric hand-dryers in the Belfast ferry terminal in 1977?

I wish I knew what we did all day; how the day un-spooled. It would still be early in the morning: the Hey-sham to Belfast crossing takes eight hours, so if we sailed at 10 p.m., as they do these days, it would only have been six in the morning at this point. Maybe we took a taxi into the city centre and found a hotel we could have breakfast in. Hotels were often targets for bombs at this time. The Europa became the most-bombed hotel in the world at one point, and if you go there today you can still – appar-ently, and a strange sort of boast – see bullet marks be-hind the reception desk. My mother wouldn't have chosen a café, though: she wouldn't have chosen anywhere small, where people would be curious at her accent, and ask questions. I'm instinctively sure of this. So let's say we made our way into the city and found somewhere to eat. It must have been an adventure for me, the fish and chips and the ferry, the overnight sea, and perhaps this sense continued, when my mother let me order sausages and bacon and breakfast muffins, and post slices of bread through the toasting machine. Or perhaps I was fractious, tired and bemused by the long journey, picking up on my mother's nervous tension. Perhaps it was raining, dreary and incessant, and my mother's carefully coaxed curls went limp again. The woman behind the desk looks at us oddly and says that breakfast is for residents only and turns us away into the chill, wet morning. There's no way of knowing. I can only surmise.

It must feel strange to be in a city you've seen so much in the papers, and in the news. The city you know your lover's from, the city where he lives. You must feel like an impostor, being there and him not knowing that you're there. Every street, every building, must seem significant. As if he's just around the corner, as if each cigarette left smouldering in an ashtray is his and he's just left the room, the air not yet settled into the shape of his leaving. You're terrified, on account of the bombs and the shootings, jumping out of your skin each time a car starts up behind you, a horn goes, but nonetheless – and the rain's let off, for now, the rainclouds thick and replenishing themselves but having a momentary break – you wander through a few of the streets, the central streets, Chichester Street and Bedford Street and Donegall Place, the square around the City Hall – and you can't resist telling your daughter to pay attention, even though she's too young to understand, because this place is in her blood. You must have fantasised about coming to live here, wondering if you could, or would, or if he'd move to London permanently, instead – would want a new start. Belfast's no place for raising kids, you think, although of course plenty of people do. He does.

In London it's easy to keep thoughts of his other family at bay but here they press close. You feel that everyone's looking at you, that people can tell, that they know. People are looking at you: fashions are more conservative here, and at least a decade behind. In your yellow maxi dress and terracotta jacket you look like an exotic bird of paradise. Perhaps it gets too much. Perhaps the rain starts again. You duck into a department store and kill time by letting your daughter ride the escalator up and down and look at toys in the toy department. You have a cup of tea here and when it's finished you order a bun, or a scone, which turns to thick paste in your mouth for the few bites you take. You've still got time to kill so you wander around some more, try to look at patterns, but you can't concentrate. Your daughter is bored, misbehaving, on the verge of a tantrum. You go back to the café and let her have her Rice Krispie bun, millionaire's shortbread, cream bun, anything to keep her quiet. You decide you'll go at ten o'clock this morning but this suddenly feels too early, so you think: half past ten, then eleven o'clock, and you watch a big clock counting down the minutes, the seconds. At eleven o'clock precisely, your make-up and hair redone for the second or third time already this morning, the crumbs brushed from your daughter's mouth, you leave the store – Robinson & Cleaver or C&A or Anderson & Macauley – and you hail a black taxi in the street and give him the scrap of paper with the address, an address you secretly copied once from the driving licence in your lover's wallet, and the driver nods and the taxi shudders into motion.

It's as close to what must have happened as anything. What happened next I do remember, though hazily. The black taxi drove through the town, down ever leafier, ever wider streets, until it dropped us outside the drive of a big, square, red-brick house set back from the road. My mother paid, we climbed out, walked down the drive.

How her heart must have been thumping.

On the doorstep, she spat in her hanky and wiped my face once more, then rang the bell.

Nobody came.

We waited; rang again. We could hear the bell echoing in the house, but no footsteps. We tried a third time, then we tried to walk around the back, but there was a locked gate in a high fence and you couldn't get through.

My mother can't have planned for this. The adrenalin must have been surging. Here she was, she'd come all this way – and her nemesis, the enemy, the woman whose heart she was going to break and whose life she was going to break up wasn't in. It was as banal as that.

We walked back down the drive to wait for the woman to come back. Something in my mother, some stubborn nugget of pride, or decorum, must have prevented her from sitting down right there, on the porch.

For a while, we stood against the wall of the house across the road. But it was raining, I was grumbling, and my mother must have worried that someone would come out and ask her what she was doing: this was the height of the Troubles, and an unknown woman, even one with a small child, standing outside a house watching another house was enough to stir up fear and paranoia. So we walked a little way down the street and took shelter in a bus stop. I don't know how long we waited there. An hour? Two? Half an hour? Two buses came past, but each time my mother said that we were waiting for a different one.

Then it happened. A third bus came by and a blonde woman got off, carrying several shopping bags, ushering a dark-haired little girl in front of her. They must have passed right by us, each party oblivious. They crossed the road and walked down the drive of the house we'd been watching – the house I didn't know was my father's house. My mother was deathly white. It must have seemed a game to me, the watching, the waiting. But – and I think this must be why I remember this episode in such detail, when I couldn't tell you about my first day at school anywhere near as closely – I suddenly realised that it wasn't a game at all. From time to time you hear people say 'the colour drained from her face' and you think it's a figure of speech, until you actually see it happen. My mother gripped my hand so tightly I cried out and then she stood up and started walking, fast, so that I had to run to keep up with her. We walked back in the direction we'd come, past the house, down the slight incline and out onto the main road, my mother like a creature possessed.

The woman, you see, had been heavily pregnant – even more pregnant than my mother. My father's wife, like his mistress, was due to give birth that autumn. Once my mother saw that – and what must it have felt like to see that, to realise? – she couldn't confront the woman. Maybe, with everything that happened later, she wished she had: but in that moment she couldn't, didn't.

We spent the rest of the day in the Ulster Museum, looking at the dinosaurs.

Alfie and I

There are too many holes in my story, I'm seeing this already; too much I just don't know. How could our mother stay with our father when he'd lied to her – when he'd kept it from her that his wife was pregnant, too? And my father: did he intend to break it off with my mother, now that his wife was pregnant again, *because* his wife was pregnant again, but when he steeled himself to do it she announced that she was pregnant as well? How must it have felt, your wife and your mistress, simultaneously, or just about, having babies? How did he keep the secrets, on both sides, and how did my mother let slip that she knew about Catriona? Did he admit it, or did she ask him outright, and pretend she had a dream, or an intuition? And what did he say, what could he possibly say? Then did she leave him, for a while? I seem to remember that. Going to my grandmother's in Yorkshire – my grandmother, a woman I was scared of, and hardly knew. I think I remember the train journey there, and the papery, powdery cheek I was supposed to kiss, and I might remember arguments and tears. Why don't I remember more? Why do I remember the trip to Ireland, and not to Yorkshire, when they both must have happened around the same time, and in similarly emotionally charged circumstances? Perhaps we didn't go to Yorkshire, at all. My mother's father was very ill by then – he'd just had the second of the series of strokes that killed him. Perhaps she hadn't told him about the pregnancy, so as not to upset him. Perhaps she hadn't told her own mother, either. They barely saw each other by now, corresponding when they did by letter or occasional fraught phone calls. It's not implausible that six months, a year, could have passed since my grandmother ventured down to London, tied as she was to her querulous, invalid husband. Then again, surely knowing her own father was so ill would be enough to make my mother brave the journey back home, to see him before he died? I just don't know: I just don't know. I wish I could ask her. Even just one of the bigger questions: did you leave my father, and for how long, and what made you go back? Was it your own mother's opprobrium, or the thought of being a single mother of two in your childhood home in the tiny village of Routh? That sounds plausible. But that, surely, is better than going back to the man who has doubly betrayed you. Surely it is? How did my father persuade her to come back to him, how, *how*? How was his life sustainable, a child and a baby with his mistress, a child and a baby with his wife? It must have felt like a ghastly nightmare, some hellish joke. For my mother, too. I don't understand, I just don't and can't. My mother would never say any more than that she loved my father: but that, surely, isn't it, or isn't enough. Love isn't an excuse, and if there's a love strong enough to surmount the things she went through: as I said at the start, it's a love of which I'm incapable.

I went to visit Alfie last night, to see if he could fill in any of the gaps. Although much of what I need to know happened before he was born, and although he's younger than me and so his memory is even more useless than mine, he was closer to our mother than I was, and I know she talked to him more, especially in the last weeks. He must know something, I thought. However small, however trivial a thing seems, it's better than the gaping blanks of knowing nothing.

But he isn't interested. He said that to me, flatly and decisive: I'm not interested in any of this, Lara. Only harm can come of it.

I didn't dare tell him I was writing all of it down. I just sat there in their nice Welwyn lounge with its 'feature wall' and too many scatter cushions, its 'tasteful' black and white photographs that look like they came with the frame, drinking my mug of Victoria-Beckham-swears-by-it pu-erh tea.

I sound mean, I know. I sound outright bitchy. Partly it's frustration. Also, his wife Danielle brings it out in me. She came in, halfway through my pleading with Alfie to rack his brains for something, anything, and she put her manicured hand on my arm and her pained, long-suffering expression on her face and said that she couldn't help but catch the gist of what we were discussing and she had to say that she agreed with Alfie, it was no good what I was doing, and perhaps I should rethink it, or what I was doing it for, and Alfie looked relieved and shifty all at the same time and said that it was no use digging dead dogs up, or something equally irrelevant.

I waited until she'd gone, back to helping the girls with their music practice, and I tried him again.

'In the last days, Alfie. She must have said something.'

I'd moved from my sofa to his, and he was pulling miserably at his chin.

'Please, Alfie. She must have let slip . . . something.'

'I don't know what you want me to say, Lara.'

'I just want you to try—'

'I've already told you. She was – confused. You know that. The way she'd just ramble.'

'But something, she must have said something. Something you didn't know, or something that stuck with you. Please, Alfie, think.'

'Why is it suddenly so important?'

One of the twins was sawing out a bowdlerised version of *Carnival of the Animals*. Alfie winced, and smiled. He wanted me to comment, but I didn't.

'You haven't drunk your tea,' he said.

'Nor have you,' I pointed out. He took a gulp and looked at me.

'Why are you like this, Lara?'

'Like what?'

'I think you must be very unhappy. I wish you'd let us . . .' He stopped; shrugged; smiled at me lopsidedly.

'Let you what, Alfie?' I said, keeping my voice even. 'You wish I'd let you what?'

'Don't do this, Lara. Help you. I wish you'd let us—'

'Help me. By having me round on Sundays and giving me double helpings of pity with lashings of pity and sprinkles of pity on top.' I knew I was behaving badly. What is it about your siblings that regresses you, brings out your worst? Half an hour with Alfie, and he was eight again, and I was twelve, and goading and loathing and envying him.

90

I took a breath. 'Sorry. I didn't mean – I just need to know. If Mum left Dad when she found out about him, about Michael.' He winced as I said the name, but I ploughed on. 'If she did, and where she went, and why she went back to him. Why it went on for a further eight years – eight years, Alfie – and what they planned to do when we were too old to be lied to any longer. And even that holiday, I've been thinking about it, and why did she agree to go in the first place? Surely she knew it would be a disaster? Do you think – because here's what I think – it was a sort of, forcing the cards? Knowing that I was turning twelve, and maybe thinking that the time had come, sort of thing, or do you think—'

'Lara.' Like our mother, Alfie rarely raised his voice, but he raised it now. His voice is too high-pitched to be raised; it sounds ridiculous. 'You have to let it go, don't you see that? We're not them. They had their lives, and we've got ours. I know – everything with, with Jeremy and that. But you've got to – and don't take this the wrong way – you've got to try. Otherwise – otherwise, Lara . . .' He was leaning forward and gripping his mug in both hands, and his thick knuckles were white and shaking. He was craning to meet my eye. I looked slowly up. His eyes were almost watering with intensity. 'Well, Danielle said it. She said it better than I did.'

'Danielle,' I said, before I could stop myself. 'How can she understand? She's not one of us.'

Alfie looked away. 'I know you've never liked her, Lara,' he said. 'But I wish you'd have more respect. Danielle's my us.'

The elephants lumbered to the end of their minuet,

squashing a few cawing swans underfoot. Neither of us said anything in the silence that followed. Alfie stood up, and gathered up our mugs. I tried to find something to say, or a way to say it. Danielle came in.

'Oh, you're still here, Lara.' Bright, artificial, tolerant. 'Freddie, the girls are dying to play you something. I'm sure they'd be thrilled if you popped up, too, Lara.'

'Thanks,' I said, and got to my feet. I was surprised to find how shaky my legs felt, as if they were turning to water beneath me. 'But I think I'd better head back. Early start tomorrow. Another time.'

I brushed the cheek she offered to me and turned to go, pretending not to notice Danielle's glances at Alfie and his almost imperceptible shakings of the head: the secret sign language of couples. I was surprised, after the way I'd behaved, when Alfie hugged me; and even more surprised at the strength of the hug, but I managed to hold it together until I was safely outside in the car.

You wouldn't recognise Alfie now, if you had known him then. Then, he was slight and fair and almost pretty, his Tintined quiff of hair and pale, translucent skin, his sandy eyelashes and blue-veined temples. Now, only in his mid-thirties, he is tall and beefy in an ungainly, apologetic way. His eyes are big and bloodhound-sad with a tendency to water, which makes them bloodshot. Though that could be the alcohol: he drinks too much, and not in an exuberant way. When Alfie drinks it is in a steady, determined, sinking-the-pints sort of way. His hair is receding rapidly at the temples and on the crown of his head, I've noticed that lately, and the little gingerish goatee he's grown since Christmas makes him look like a used-car salesman. Or, I suppose, the estate agent that he is. That Alfie, shy, imaginative little Alfie, should end up an estate agent, of all things – although, then again, you don't need to be a psychologist to see how directly it's related to everything that happened after our father died.

I shouldn't deride it so much, I know. He helped our mother buy a house near him in Welwyn and after Jeremy he helped me, too. Besides, who am I to talk? An agency carer with barely an A level to my name; I'm not exactly setting the world on fire. You look at your sibling, though – the little brother you loved so much and protected and fought for as well as with and you think: your life wasn't meant to be like this, either, and you're unhappy because of it. Danielle is a sharp, pointy-chinned woman who doesn't let anything pass her by. She does yoga and Pilates; is always on some diet or other; gets her roots done every six weeks and her nails every fortnight. I'm always terrified she'll leave Alfie. He adores her, hopelessly, and the twins, who make a game of teasing him and inventing elaborate stories and scenarios at his expense. He takes it as affection but it's all too plain to see that in a few years, when they're teenagers, their friendly disdain for Daddy will become derision, and eventually they'll despise him. Alfie thinks I'm wrong for trying to uncover our past: he's just as wrong, I think, for trying to bury it.

We had a childhood that made us a lot closer, I think, than most sisters and brothers. Our mother didn't have many friends, and the two of us picked up on this: we rarely invited people over, either, and instead relied on ourselves, our tight little unit. Perhaps we sensed that we were different from other families we knew, and we closed ranks. We did everything together, Alfie and I. We'd shared a bedroom all our lives: even at the time of our father's death, when I was twelve and he was eight, we were still sharing one room, with bunk beds. Our room was small – big enough for the beds and a wardrobe, little else – and airless in summer. I'd started to hate sharing that bedroom with Alfie. Since that Easter time, when I'd begun to notice things weren't quite right, I'd become hyperconscious of the changes in my body, too, of the small, hard, aching lumps of my breasts budding; of the soft, light brown hair like the pelt of an animal furring my underarms; of the sparse, crunchy twists of pubic hair. One night I was climbing the ladder to the top bunk, knickerless under my knee-length nightie, when I felt Alfie's curious gaze. I turned and challenged him and he replied, with all the matter-of-fact simplicity of a seven-year-old, 'You've got hair on your bottom, you know.' I jumped down and slapped him, hard, and he cried and I lay awake most of the night burning with embarrassment and hating both of us. It felt wrong – mortifyingly wrong – to be sharing such confined space with my younger brother. Other girls in my class had bedrooms of their own, or bedrooms they shared with their sister, where there was no Lego or train tracks or boys' socks underfoot, where you could sit and crimp your hair or paint your nails or make origami fortune-tellers, pretend to fancy *Home and Away* stars in *Big!* and read aloud the personality quizzes and problem pages in discarded, older sisters' copies of

Just Seventeen. When I built up the courage to raise the issue with our mother she just went quiet and wouldn't look at me.

I understand better, now, her reaction: what, after all, could she possibly do? My father, and of course I had no idea of any of this, had already lied to his wife about why he needed to move from his one-bedroom mansion-block flat to a bigger place around the corner. I think – I remember asking my mother about this, after he died – he made up some story about structural problems, or one of the people opposite wanting to buy up two flats and knock them together, and making him an offer he couldn't refuse. How, though, could he invent, without raising suspicion, an excuse for needing an even larger, three-bedroomed apartment?

As I write all of this I realise yet again how little I know about any of it. The sheer logistics of it, maintaining two families, two entire lives! How did he explain electricity and gas bills, which would have been extortionate, given that the flat was only meant to be in use when he was there, which was approximately two long weekends a month and a couple of fortnights at Easter and in the summer? Did he have separate accounts? I suppose he must have done. Lied about what he was earning, siphoned off some here and there for us. He used to give our mother cash, I remember: a folded white envelope every time he saw us. Even cash leaves traces, though. Did his accountant back in Belfast, the one who helped him with his taxes from his private practice, know about his double life? And she, Catriona Connolly, did she really have no idea? Did she never want to come to

London, escape the tensions and troubles in Belfast? He owned a flat, after all – they owned a flat, rather. It was – the audacity of it – held in her name. How did he put her off coming, all those years, because she must have wanted to – mustn't she? The children must have, at least. Wanted to see the Tower of London and Madame Tussauds. The Egyptian mummies in the British Museum and the Dungeon and Hamleys and all the rest of it. How did he put them off, and how on earth did they never suspect? Everything loops back to it, again and again, no matter what other stories I try to tell. The banalities of it all, the practicalities, the layers and layers of lies and counter-lies and supporting lies, the sheer balancing act of it all, temples of playing cards. And yet it went on for more than twelve years, the whole of my life until he died. Would it have come out in some other way, if it hadn't died that November? Would I have been the catalyst?

I often think that I might. Our flat on Eardley Crescent was on the second floor of a terraced house, bigger than Allenby Mansions where we'd moved from, but it was starting to feel small, especially when my father was with us. In the summertime, as I've said, Alfie and I would go out to play in Brompton Cemetery and if it was rainy we'd get a bus to the cinema. But on the coldest, darkest November or February nights when it was lashing down with rain and besides, we had homework, I'd wish with every fibre of my being that there was somewhere else to go. We'd be sitting in the living room with the television on, and our parents would be in their bedroom – our father would have just arrived – and without discussing it we'd know and hate what they were doing. We never said

a word to each other: just sat there, hot and stiff and embarrassed, and occasionally turned the volume up louder
on whatever we were watching.

So it had been building, anyway, but since Fuengirola
and learning the terrible secret of our family, I had been
wanting my own space, my own privacy, with an intensity I don't think I can put into words. I'd stopped talking
to my father. I don't think, between the start of August
when we saw him again and the start of November when
we saw him for the last time, I exchanged more than
a few words with him. Certainly none of my own volition. I took a perverse sort of delight in staring straight
through him – or else I'd use a trick we played on sup-
ply teachers at school, where you focused on the tip of
their left ear rather than meeting their eye. It's surprisingly unsettling, if you've never tried it. The victim can't
meet your eye, whatever they do, and it's not obvious
enough for them to realise you're playing a trick on them.
I took a seething, tight pleasure in doing this. If I had
to – my mother threatening me with being grounded, or
Alfie begging – I'd speak to our father in a monotone,
blanking all traces of myself or emotion from my voice.
He tried, several times, to talk to me or to get me on my
own – in my bedroom, or out for a walk – but I shut
him out. I think a conflicted part of me enjoyed it, the
whole and sustained focus of his attention on me. I could
have threatened to contact his wife and other children
and blow his secrets into the open – in bed at night I rehearsed, over and over, what I would say – but I never
did it. I knew I could, though, and I enjoyed the power. It
gave me a different power at school, too. I'd always been

quiet and unremarkable in my primary school, the child whose name teachers struggled to remember on parents' evening. Starting secondary in September, with the fury and force of the summer's revelations behind me, made me powerful in a way that other children sensed, even if they didn't understand. It made me reckless – made me stop caring what teachers or other people thought, made me stop trying to please people or to be obedient. I fell in, almost immediately, with the bad crowd in my year, the ones who even at twelve were already drinking and smoking and sniffing tubes of glue squeezed into plastic Londis bags, and although I was never the leader of any of the cliques I was never their target because they somehow knew that they had no way to hurt me. Often, that autumn, and especially when my father was over, I would spend the evenings roaming the streets and the parks with my new-found friends and come home deliberately stinking of cigarettes, just daring my parents or Alfie to say something. They never did. They felt out of their depth, perhaps, or guilty, or perhaps they were hoping the whole thing would blow over or settle down; that my rage would work itself out. And my mother: was she still, endlessly, yet again, drearily hoping that now things would resolve themselves; that now we knew, my father would have to act, make a decision, that something would have to change?

I've often wondered, increasingly so in recent years, what effect that summer and the subsequent autumn had on Alfie. It's easy to see my rebellion: it's almost textbook. The falling-in-with-a-bad-crowd, the drink and the

drugs, the warnings at school, the failed exams. I even –
and I regret this almost every day – destroyed our family photo albums, stacking the leatherette volumes in a
carrier bag and taking them down to the dustbin en-
closure. I put them out the evening before the collec-
tion was due, and for the whole of that night I enjoyed
knowing that nobody had realised they were gone. It was
my father's first visit to us after Fuengirola, and although
there'd been tears and apologies all around I'd somehow
gleaned that nothing had changed or imminently was going to: not he leaving his wife nor our mother leaving
him. If I'd changed my mind, I could have retrieved them
– I'd put them in a Hamleys bag, with its distinctive rows
of red and black soldiers, which stood out among the
smelly black sacks. I wondered if I would: almost did.
But I didn't, and in the morning I watched the binmen
in their stained woollen hats and fingerless gloves hurling
the rubbish into the jaws of their truck and I felt hot and
faint with what I'd done. Even that, though, didn't make
my mother shout or hit me: she just shut herself in her
room and wouldn't answer my knocking. Alfie just stared
at me with big, scared eyes; flinched when I moved too
near him. At seven and a half he was old enough to understand in principle about our father's other family, but
young enough still to trust in the adults and believe that
they'd make things all right in the end. If my reaction was
loud and outward, bolshie and bravado, his was inward:
he became even quieter than ever, I remember, and I
hated him for it. I'd come in from my nights out and clat-
ter about our bedroom, deliberately trying to wake him
up so he'd complain and I could shout and Mum would

have to get involved, but he'd just lie there, eyes closed though I knew he was awake. Sometimes I'd pry his eyelids open and he'd wriggle away and try to keep under his shield of sleep, and when he couldn't pretend any longer he'd just lie there watching me, or watching the slats on the bunk above when I yelled at him to keep his eyes to himself, and he'd never say a word. The meeker and quieter he was, the more he shied and skirted round me, the more I loathed him and the worse I behaved. To our mother, too, who didn't, or couldn't, or wouldn't say anything: who would just hug Alfie to her and plead at me with silent eyes and weep, weep, silent and pathetic until I hated her for it.

Later events, after our father died, brought Alfie and me together again, but we each, as soon as we could, escaped the trenches and each other. For years we rarely saw one another, until the last months of our mother's illness brought us back together. Alfie's help when Jeremy left me brought us closer, to the extent that I started going round on Sundays for a while, but we don't quite work like we did as children. Maybe we realise, when we're with each other, how damaged each of us is: something that when we're alone or with others we can disguise or ignore.

I've been skirting around it but should write, now, about what came next.

Sunday 24th November 1985

My father died on Sunday 24th November 1985. You like to think that you'd know these things, you'd somehow feel it: but we didn't, not for at least another two days. He'd been with us for Alfie's birthday, his eighth, at the start of the month. We'd gone to the Hard Rock Cafe and I'd scowled at our father as he flirted with the waitress – bantered, he would have said, but for me nothing was neutral now – and I'd stabbed at my burger and said I was becoming vegetarian. I'd stopped calling him Daddy, then, and called him Patrick instead. I said he didn't deserve the title, and he didn't try to argue. My mother started to cry. Alfie begged me to be a family, just for his birthday. It was a terrible night. I sometimes wonder if it was because of that night that our father didn't come over the following fortnight, as he was meant to do. I said this to my mother, once, shortly afterwards, and she said, Of course not, don't be silly, his schedule had just changed, that was all. But I could see as I said it something quavering in her eyes, some failure to say it with utter conviction. I felt, then, for years, that I was somehow responsible, that he'd died as a result of the force of my hate.

How he actually died was as follows. There'd been an IRA mortar bomb attack on an RUC barracks out in the country. They timed it for a Sunday night, when it wouldn't be expected, when people would be at ease in their temporary accommodation inside the barrack walls. The weather was terrible that night. It had been pouring down with rain all day, relentless, and when night fell the winds picked up. Branches were falling from trees, the rain was lashing, and any creature that had a home to go to was in it. They struck just after 10 p.m., and killed two men, wounding several others, some critically. My father was paged to the hospital, but the ambulances couldn't get through – a tree had fallen – and so it was arranged that a helicopter would go to airlift the two most critical cases to hospital. Time had elapsed by this stage, and my father was worried for the men, one of whom had lost a leg, so he went in the helicopter to the barracks. One of the men had died by the time they got there, but in a makeshift operating theatre, my father and the barracks doctor and the paramedic managed to stabilise the other, stanching the flow of blood and binding the wounds, and then they transferred him into the helicopter to take him back to the hospital for the life-saving surgery he'd need. Three minutes after take-off – and nobody's quite sure how this happened, the storm, the dark, the night, pilot error, equipment failure – the helicopter crashed down, killing instantly the pilot, the paramedic, the patient, and my father.

It was a tragedy in a time and place of daily tragedies. It was, of course, reported extensively on the news: but our mother hated the news, especially news of Northern Ireland, so we didn't see it in the papers or hear it on the radio the following day. Alfie and I were at school that day: it was just a normal, boring Monday. Our mother stayed in; cleaned the flat; read her novel; sewed a new dress she was making. If she'd gone out – even just to Mr Patel's – she might have seen or heard something, but she didn't. The Harley Street practice must have heard: but they had no idea that the nurse who'd worked there briefly, all those years ago, was still involved with one of their doctors. It wasn't until the Tuesday, and the evening, that we had the first intimations that something was wrong. These were the days before mobile phones, and so my parents went days without communicating. They'd spoken on Wednesday, when my father said he wouldn't be coming over; they'd spoken again on Friday evening, briefly. He rarely phoned over the weekend, so our mother thought nothing of it when she didn't hear from him on Saturday, Sunday, Monday. By Tuesday she started to worry, but it was the low-level, constant worry that maybe he'd been caught in a bomb scare, or maybe Catriona had discovered something, the maybes that she had to battle to suppress. Then on Tuesday night, Alfie left the television on after watching Children's BBC and a short report on *Newsround* mentioned a helicopter crash following an attack on a barracks in Northern Ireland's Co. Fermanagh. None of us were watching it, but my mother, making dinner, heard it in the background – *the four passengers, including the pilot and a survivor of the earlier attach, as well as a paramedic and a surgeon, were instantly killed, bringing the total number of fatalities so far this year . . .* Something in her, she says, twinged. The news report ended; she called to Alfie to switch off the television, and she finished preparing our dinner. Then she sat us down to eat it and went into her bedroom, where she scrolled through every radio station she could think of, the volume down low, in the hope of hearing more news. When she found none, she came back into the living room and calmly said she was nipping to the shop for a moment. She put on her coat, laced up her shoes, crooked her handbag on her arm and left. Alfie and I looked at each other, shrugged, and continued wolfing our chips and beans or whatever our dinner was that evening. A few minutes later, she came back with an armful of papers. The incident was on none of the front pages and she hadn't stopped to read any of them at Mr Patel's. She had the *Evening Standard*, the *Guardian*, the *Times*, the *Daily Telegraph*, the *Sun* and two or three others. She didn't say a word. We began to realise that something was up. Without taking off her coat or outdoor shoes, her bag still hanging from her arm, she sat down and started going through the first paper in the pile – the *Times* – scanning and discarding each page. We looked at each other; looked at her. Then she stopped. She took a long, shaky breath, and for a moment was completely still. And then she dropped the paper she was holding and started whipping through the others, frantically, ripping the pages, as Alfie and I stood watching. And somehow, we knew.

Strange, given the detail with which I remember everything else: but those first few hours, those first couple of days, are a blur, a blank. I suppose it must have been shock. I don't remember crying. I must have done. I remember not going to school, and one of my teachers coming around. One of Alfie's friends' mothers came round, too – that's right – with a baby that dribbled strings of drool over my jumper when I was given it to hold. Those were all our visitors, I think. Our mother didn't have any friends to rally round – how could she, when so much of her life was so secret? She told acquaintances that her husband worked much of his time in Ireland, but it wasn't safe for the children, so we lived here. That was her line, and beyond it she kept people at a distance. Any closer and they'd have begun to realise that something was not quite right with our family, our setup. Did a lady from next door bring around a casserole? It sounds plausible. But I don't really remember. Everything else is hazy. What I remember most from those days is a moment from that very first night – which for his real family wasn't, of course, the first night but the third. I remember sitting there in the waste of newspapers while Mum phoned our father's Belfast number, his home phone number. From the babble of voices in the background as the phone was answered, she knew there hadn't been a mistake. When she put the phone down she said: They thought I was a reporter, and they asked me to leave the family alone to let them grieve.

We went to Belfast for the funeral. It was held the following Monday, the second of December: Catholic funeral masses may not take place on Sundays during Advent. We would slip in once the service had started, our mother had decided. It came out later, who we were – *that* we were – but it hadn't yet, and as far as our mother knew, the Connollys knew nothing about us.

So, Alfie's first time in Belfast; my and our mother's second. We flew there, first thing in the morning, and our mother booked us return flights for the same evening: she couldn't face a night in that squalid, hateful city. I remember how grey and wet it was, how raw the air, how clammy. The darkness of the huddled buildings; the darkness of the pavements; the dour faces of the people in the streets. The great blanket of clouds in the sky, and no sign of the sun. We waited in a greasy spoon for the time to pass and the service to begin. Alfie and I were in our school uniforms, his light grey, mine black, the soberest clothes we had. Our mother was in a black skirt and coat and a low-brimmed black hat to hide her face. She made us order full English breakfasts – or rather, Ulster fries – so that we'd have a reason to be in the café. She made us eat them, too: I remember the gagging feeling of chewing on spongy clumps of sausage and sodden fatty bread. The prickle of fizzy orange in the back of my nose; sharp, like tears.

The streets just off the main road looked familiar from all the news broadcasts we'd seen: small dirty rows of terraced houses, many with bricked-up doorways and windows. Rubble and mesh and women in headscarves, heads down. An Army patrol. A thin-looking dog, missing an eye. The shivery feeling of being watched.

In the end, my mother's nerve deserted her and we didn't go to the funeral, after all. We sat on a wall by a derelict, bombed-out building within sight of the back entrance of the church, and we watched the impassive, soot-stained building, and my mother held Alfie's hand but I took mine back. The memory of being with her that other time in Belfast, watching a house from outside, waiting, outside of the story, came back to me stronger than ever before. We sat there for perhaps half an hour; it's hard to tell. Twice a patrolling officer asked us what our business was and our mother said that we were meant to be at the funeral but it had been too much for her little boy and so we were having a breather out here, waiting for the rest of our party. I remember being impressed at how fluidly, how plausibly, the lies came from her tongue. Then again, she'd had our lifetimes of it.

None of us knew how long a Catholic Mass would be; how long before we'd have to leave. At one point, our mother – agonised, flitting back and forth with her decisions – decided that she wanted to look in, to set foot – literally, just that – in the building. We watched as she jogged across the street and up the steps and round the building; disappeared; returned a moment later, flushed, saying that it was ending and we had to go, and that was that.

A day or so later, it came out that our father had a second family. I still, to this day, don't know quite how. Catriona Connolly clearing her husband's office (do consultants have their own offices?) at the hospital? Or his locker; finding a photograph, some kind of evidence? A well-meaning colleague, who knew or had gathered more than he should, thinking he was doing her – or us – a kindness by taking her aside, a quiet word in her ear, about his suspicions? Had our father ever let anything slip to his mother – our grandmother – or to his sister? Did they know, or guess, or know enough to ask questions? Were there documents there shouldn't have been, or bills, or statements that didn't add up? Had Catriona suspected anything before, and put away the hunch, high on a shelf beyond everyday reach? However it happened, it happened: we were discovered, and it was all over the media, at least in Ireland. The Two Faces of the Plastic Surgeon, Dr Jekyll and Mr Hyde, the tabloids were gleeful. Somehow, Catriona got or was given our number, and she rang one afternoon to speak to our mother. I don't know what was said. Our mother took the phone into her bedroom, stretching the cable under the door. We listened, but all we could hear her say was Yes, No, Yes, I'm sorry, Off and on, Thirteen years; our lives, her story, apologetic syllables. Somehow, too, the journalists found out our address. We were photographed leaving the flat in Eardley Crescent: an unflattering one of our mother, her face hard and old-looking; Alfie's and my eyes blacked out with strips. That was when she said it, and who knows if it was just defiance, but it has always seemed to me that she was telling her truth: *I would do it all again, I wouldn't trade anything, not even the outcome, not even if I knew the outcome right from the start.*

If it had happened earlier – if the truth about us had come out before the funeral, say – there might have been some sort of reconciliation. No: 'reconciliation' is too strong a word, but we might at least have been admitted to the funeral, and had a chance or a reason to meet our counterparts, and to meet the grandmother and aunt and cousins we'd never had. As it was, and with my mother's words in capitals in the tabloids, Catriona Connolly declared she wanted nothing to do with us, ever, and I must say understandably so.

North End Road

Three months after my father dies, we're informed that we have to move house: Catriona is putting Eardley Crescent – which is held in her name, and left to her by the terms of our father's will – on the market. They talked once – my mother says – about his making provision for us in his will; it would have been shortly after Alfie was born; for whatever reason or reasons, he never got around to doing it. I've never been able to understand that. I can't make myself believe that it was callous, a cruel sort of denial of us. So what was it? Sheer negligence? I can't believe that, either. Was it practicality – his wife's signature needed on any changes in the will? Was his solicitor a family friend, someone he couldn't confess or expose himself to? Was it that when he was back in Belfast we faded slightly, and such matters seemed less pressing? Whatever it was, I can't understand it, or him, and I can't forgive him. In our savings accounts were a few hundred pounds each; nothing. He could have made provision for us, somehow. The only hard, cold fact I have is that he didn't: and in the end that overrides the reasons why.

It's February, and bitter. The plane trees are black and slimy-trunked; squalid heaps of semi-putrefied leaves nestle round dustbin enclosures. Pigeons, sodden puffs of tufts and fleas, hop baleful-eyed along dank pavements, looking even more pestilent than usual. Umbrellas broken-boned and abandoned, useless against the driving winds. After school, I sit for hours at our living-room window, watching the birds and the newspapers and the chip-wrappings blown to and fro in the road, hideous under the watery orange light of the street lamps. I watch people swarming home from work, huddled neckless in their long dark coats. The grimy scraps of the day, fag-ends and litter, gusting in their wake.

A London affiliate of Catriona's solicitors comes to make a survey of the flat and handle proceedings. Then an estate agent. Alfie, Mum and I sit out each visit in silence, lined up on the sofa: three pairs of eyes watching mutely, stonily, accusing, ashamed. We think they think we're tenants, but we can't be sure. The solicitor is a brisk, efficient, apologetic man with a slight astigmatism and thinning hair. The estate agent is a thin, gangly, baby-faced man with the worst case of acne I've ever seen. I imagine him scraping his razor over his cheeks each morning, slicing the heads of competing clusters of pustules, liquid seeping. I draw a comic strip for Alfie, with them as the villains. The fourth or fifth potential buyer shown around agrees to take the place, but at a sum far under the asking price: he knows, or guesses, that the vendor wants a quick sale. Done and dusted – I remember the solicitor's phrase – as soon as possible. Those are his instructions.

He doesn't look us in the eye. He doesn't believe we're tenants, after all. He must have seen the newspapers from Belfast, the photo of our mother and her defiant words. She should have been repentant and apologetic, begging forgiveness, but she wasn't, wouldn't.

Our mother is working all hours at the moment, to try to keep us afloat. Her main job is as an auxiliary nurse at the Charing Cross Hospital in Hammersmith. She's started walking the forty minutes there and back to save on the bus fare. Only if she's on a late shift and we beg her will she agree to take a night bus up Lillie Road past Normand Park, where the junkies and drug-dealers hang out after dark. Alfie begs her, and I beg her, too. I have a weird, unshakeable feeling that I somehow killed my father – as if I willed it, caused it – and I'm suddenly, irrationally, terrified for our mother now because I've hated her as well these last few months. She says she takes the bus. We hope we believe her. Auxiliary nursing – bed-making, bedpan-slopping, washing and dressing and cleaning sick and wiping arses – doesn't pay, even when you're working back-to-back shifts and emergency cover. So for the past few weeks our mother's been trying to find extra work cleaning houses. We hate this. There are cards up on the windows of the local newsagent, the Indian takeaway and the library, the café opposite West Brompton Tube station, and we are mortified: for ourselves, and for her. She hasn't had many takers, though, and for this we are grateful beyond belief. People don't like a middle-aged white woman, so obviously fallen on hard times, mopping their floors and scrubbing at their spattered loos. It makes them uneasy: it's too close to home.

She doesn't know how we are going to manage, now. Her face is tight and thin and lined these days. It's a cliché, but it's true: she looks easily ten years older. Perhaps her mother could help, or her sister Helen: but she's too proud to tell them how bad things are. Besides, it's not as if any of them could be any immediate, practical solace. Our grandmother lives in Beverley now, on a modest pension in a small two-bedroom house, and Helen has married a Canadian and moved to Toronto. While Mum's on lates I creep into her room and read Aunt Helen's occasional, slapdash letters, bold sloping writing on flimsy airmail paper, and I wonder if our mother thinks of going there. *You guys should come!* she writes, and *The kids would love it!* and she's only talking about a holiday, but I think: what if? A new start: a whole new beginning, a whole half-world away. These days I wonder what we might have been like had we slipped our skins and become Canadians. I think of our other-selves, living other-lives, and the thought makes me oddly sad. Mourning the loss of something you've never had: how absurd. How do you know, I tell myself, that things would have been any better? They might have been worse; we might have ended up doubly, triply exiled from ourselves and our previous life. But yet: even now, I can't help it, help wondering if that was a turning we missed, and these days, after Jeremy, it descends on me with a new intensity.

Perhaps, it occurs to me with a sudden and nasty stab, that's ageing. I see it all the time with the elderly people I look after. All of them, almost without exception, mourning their other selves. Haunted by their ghost-lives, the people they could or should have been. I feel too young to feel like this. But the truth is I'm almost forty, childless and alone, with little hope of writing myself out of the script and the story I'm trapped in.

All I can do is keep going.

We didn't go to Canada, and perhaps it was only my imagination that we ever might have. One day, the squinting solicitor phones and says that his client Mrs Connolly has informed him that we will be receiving half the proceeds of the sale, once tax and duties have been cleared, in a lump sum. It's on condition, he stresses, that my mother does not contact or attempt to contact Mrs Connolly again, ever. That my mother does not speak to any member of the media about our personal circumstances, should there at some future time be approaches made or offers effected. These criteria, he finishes, apply from the tendering of the offer, and any communications whatsoever should be made through the official channel, i.e. him.

He doesn't know – or perhaps he does – that two Irish Sunday papers have already asked our mother to tell her story, and she's told both of them to fuck off: that her life and her children's lives are not a carcass to be picked over.

I don't know, and I have always wondered, what prompted Catriona Connolly to make that decision. She was – is – a devout Catholic, as far as I can tell. Was it conscience? A sudden impulse to do the charitable thing? Or was it the advice of her solicitors that we might have been entitled to a portion of her late husband's estate: a sort of squatters' rights in his life, as it were, and this was a pre-emptive gesture? An attempt to avert a long, tangled, drawn-out court case? I've subsequently, casually, taken hypothetical advice on this and it seems that we may indeed have been entitled. The Inheritance (Provision for

Family and Dependants) Act suggests that we could have had a course of action: especially if our father's will did not contain an explicit clause defining 'children' as 'legitimates'. Nobody, so far as I know, ever suggested to our mother that she should take legal advice. I've always wondered why she didn't. Perhaps her shame kept her silent: the thought of our names being dragged through the courts, our business being known to everyone she knew. Except that doesn't chime: how, now, after everything, could our mother be felled by shame? Unless my father's death created a vacuum into which all the guilt and shame at bay for years came rushing. Or perhaps it wasn't shame but shame's opposite, pride. Perhaps she was too proud to ask for anything, to be seen to be grovelling.

Back and forth you go, back and forth, trying to reason, trying to know. Always it's useless. How can you ever begin to enter into another person's head, thoughts, fears, being?

Our mother's face, when she put down the phone, was white. She'd been asleep, snatching two hours between her day shift and a night shift she'd agreed to cover. Her hair was disarrayed, birds'-nested from its slept-in pleat. I noticed, not for the first time, how grey it was becoming. She was only thirty-five: younger than I am, now. The skin-bags beneath her eyes, pools of brown; her face, unarranged by sleep and flaccid with shock, swelling swiftly into a complicated relief. The share of the proceeds, she repeated, as if she was tasting the words for herself, would not be enough to buy another flat, but it could certainly be the mainstay of our rent for some years, if we were careful, and the start of a proper savings account for each of us.

Alfie nudged towards her. I stayed sitting in the doorway, where we'd come to watch and earwig when we'd realised that this was no ordinary conversation.

'We're going to be OK,' she said, and then, her accent slipping back into Yorkshire as she reached for Alfie, 'No need to be afleyed, love. We're going to be OK now.'

'The whole flat is ours,' Alfie said. 'Not half of it. She's never even been here.'

Our mother pulled him tight to her, and looked at me over his head, and I looked away.

We move house a few weeks later. It's the start of April, and blustery. The wind whips my long hair across my face and into my mouth and eyes as I stagger down the steps with the final boxes and bin bags of our things. Alfie is guarding them, our pile of possessions, heaped higgledy-piggledy on the pavement by the railings. He looks like a refugee from somewhere, so skinny and pale, his big eyes darting, his chapped bitten lips. He is a refugee from somewhere, I think. We all are. Refugees from our life.

Another nurse from the Charing Cross has offered to help us: her husband is a minicab driver. He arrives in his battered car to take us and our bin bags and boxes to our new home. He is West African – Nigerian, I think – and his tinny car radio is bleating out Fela Kuti in between bursts of static. We load in as much as possible. He ties our mattresses onto the roof by looping rope through the windows and round, then our mother gets into the front, and we hand her the fragile things – a couple of framed pictures, the pot of spindly honesty – and the car sets off. Alfie and I are to stay on the pavement with the rest of the things and they'll come back for us. We each sit on a sack of clothes, beanbag-style, not saying a word. The gusty wind cuts easily through my sweatshirt. I am wearing a counterfeit Fruit of the Loom sweatshirt – a last-minute Christmas present bought, I know, at the Saturday street market – and a plaid skirt with leggings and slouch socks and thin-soled plimsolls. The damp chill of the ground seeps through my shoes and into my very bones. I hunch my knees to my chest, tug my skirt down like a tent, tuck my chin under the neck of my sweatshirt. Alfie has picked up a stick and is dipping it in a puddle to draw pictures in the road. I watch him for a while and realise he's not drawing pictures but writing his initials, over and over, until the square of pavement is dark.

Our mother comes back for us sooner than I expected. We load another batch, this time lashing the bed-frames on top, heaving the dismantled dining table-top into the boot. The car drives off, open boot bobbing as if it's laughing. The third time, we manage to fit most of the remaining things into the car, and the fourth time there's room for all three of us to squeeze in, with Alfie on my lap. The smell of the car is pungent and stale; Fela is still blaring and the passenger door beside me is tied on with string and masking tape. Alfie's buttocks are bony in my lap and I jab him with my elbow to get him to shift. He twists back to look at me, bemused. For good measure, I pinch him. He doesn't so much as whimper.

It takes less than five minutes to drive to our new home. Right along Lillie Road, past West Brompton station, then right again down North End Road. You could walk it in fifteen – ten – minutes. (Except I never do: I never go back. Even walking Alfie to and from school, I make us take a circuitous route, so that we don't have to pass the places we used to live, as if those places are also a time, which is over now.)

'It's almost', says our mother, 'as if we're not moving at all, isn't it?'

Neither Alfie nor I reply. I'm not used to feeling sorry for my mother – hating her is much easier – and the emotions swirl uncomfortably in my stomach.

It had taken her days and days of searching to find us a new home. It needed to be roughly in the same area, for our schools and her hospital – and also, I suppose, to keep some notion of continuity in our lives. She must have walked miles, on the trail of private ads in *Loot* magazine and the flats advertised in spidery, misspelt writing on cards in newsagents' and dry-cleaners' windows, before she found one that would do and we could afford.

The nurse's husband double-parks, flicks his hazard lights on.

'Well, this is us,' our mother says, her voice too bright. She jangles the set of keys hanging from her thumb.

We crane to look through the steamed-up window. The nurse's husband gets out and helps our mother unload our things from the good door, so that we're free to climb out.

'Ah'll help you take dese last things in,' he says, his accent good-natured and thick.

'There's no need,' our mother says, and I wonder now

if she was embarrassed for us, or for him, about to see my and Alfie's faces.

He insists. 'Eh, waht ah you talking about?' he tuts, and he takes the keys from our mother and smiles a big, gleaming smile at us, then slings a bin bag over each shoulder and walks towards one of the houses.

I shove Alfie out and clamber after him. We're standing in front of a dilapidated row of three-storey houses, boxy bay windows and rotting windowsills, peeling paint. The nurse's husband has gone into one of the houses and we take a few faltering steps in each direction. The doorway is clogged with litter: Coca-Cola and crumpled Special Brew cans, wilted crisp packets, two, three, four used condoms. The window on the first floor is smashed in and covered with a plywood board. I take a step back and realise I'm standing in a spattered starfish of vomit.

'Well go on,' our mother says, and there is an edge to her voice.

Inside, the hallway is tobacco-coloured, with rotting hessian carpets and sooty, cracked mirrors. It smells of damp – of cabbage – of urine. We stumble in, past a brown door on the right – the ground-floor flat – and up the stairs. We, our mother tells us, are in the first-floor flat.

'The one with the broken windows?' Alfie asks, and our mother says she's sure the landlord will get them fixed in no time. Even in the midst of my shock and confusion I can tell she's lying. Our flat in Eardley Crescent was shabby around the edges, but it was light, and airy, and elegant. This flat is dim and filthy and smells of what

I come to learn is a quiet, insidious sort of despair. Our belongings are piled in the centre of the front room. The nurse's husband claps his hands together, then shakes mine and Alfie's, formally, and wishes us good luck. He leaves – we listen to his heavy footsteps going down the stairs, and I think to myself that the noise is like nails being hammered into a coffin. And then we're alone, the three of us, in our new home, in our new life.

Those first few minutes in the flat in North End Road are as clear to me as if they happened this afternoon. Alfie grabbed my hand and I let him, squeezing his sticky little paw in mine. We looked, saucer-eyed, around. It must, once upon a time, have been a respectable house. The first-floor window, like the ground-floor window directly below, was a square bay. The ceiling was reasonably high, though drooping, and there was a crumbling cluster of decorative mouldings in the centre and around the edges. One strip of the room had been cut off with a thrown-up plywood partition, to create a galley kitchen with grimy walls and peeling lino, crusted with grease. The bathroom – a toilet and slimy plastic shower cubicle – was at the end of a narrow hallway. Nothing happened when you pulled the cord for light, but even in the watery light that came from the small dirty window we could see black speckled mould growing on the walls and in between the shower's tiles. And then the bedrooms. The bedrooms were through the living room – the whole 'flat' was in reality two reception rooms, which had been sectioned off into separate spaces with cheap, flimsy walls. Only one of them – the one our mother quickly said could be ours – had a window, overlooking an alleyway and some bins. Each room was barely big enough for a double bed: our wardrobes would have to go along a wall of the living room.

'If you think, yeah, that I'm going to share with Alfie, then you're wrong. You share with Alfie. I don't know any almost-thirteen-year-old that has to share with her piss-pants little brother.'

As I said before, I'd got lippy – our mother's word – since the summer. But I didn't say those words, and for that I am grateful: I think our mother might have broken, there and then on the scuzzy floor, and never got herself up again.

Instead, with Alfie still attached, like some sort of mute, drifting sea creature, I trailed back out, did another tour, as if we might have missed something; as if our mother might suddenly realise we were in the wrong place. There might have been, please God, please please God, or Jesus or angels or anyone, a mix-up with the keys, or something, anything . . .

'We'll make it nice,' our mother said, and I realised to my horror that she was pleading with me over Alfie's head. 'Of course it needs a bit of a clean, and with our stuff all bundled like this . . . but we'll make it nice, Lara, won't we? Won't we, Alfie?'

'I'm hungry,' Alfie said.

'Shut up,' I said.

'But I am. I'm starving.'

'Well,' our mother said, 'do you fancy fried chicken, pizza, Chinese, or Indian?' She swept her arm in the direction of the road outside. The opposite side was a row of fast-food places, pawnshops, credit unions, massage parlours. She started to laugh. Her laugh was too high-pitched to be a real laugh.

'Mum,' I said. '*Mum.*'

She stopped as suddenly as she'd started.

'When are we going to start?' I said.

The frames of our bunk bed and our mother's bed were jumbled up in a heap in the living room. She squatted down; picked up a leg and a couple of slats, looked at them. It had taken her and Mr Jarvis from the basement flat in Eardley Crescent the whole morning to disassemble them. So we hauled the mattresses into the bedrooms and for the first few nights, until she begged the sleazy Turkish landlord – who insisted on kissing her and me in greeting, missing my cheek and sliming his rubbery mouth on the side of my lips – to help us build the beds again, we slept like that, in sleeping bags, like campers. As if the situation was only temporary.

I knew, and I tried fiercely to tell myself that night, lying there listening to the dull roar of traffic, and the incessant sirens, and the thumps and thuds and yells of fights outside the takeaways, and the blaring music from cars with their windows down, and the scratching in the skirting board beside my head that was mice, not rats, mice, not rats (*I will not cry, I will not cry*), that many people in the world – many people in London, in the North End Road, even – lived in worse conditions: in far worse, and far more humbling conditions. Of course we got it cleaned up, and painted, the window got fixed. A few months later, my mother bought a fold-out sofa bed for the living room and she slept there, so that Alfie and I could have a bedroom each. So writing this now, I'm reminded of that Monty Python sketch: well, we lived in a paper bag in a septic tank for three months. The North End Road was a fine place to live: it was close to parks, it had – still has – a vibrant street market every day but Sunday; bakeries, pound shops. I'd gladly live there now. So I'm going to stop now. Suffice to say, that first April night felt as if life as we knew it was truly over.

In many ways, it was. This has been a memoir of my childhood, and that first day in North End Road, my father dead, exiled from our family home, exiled from the notion that we ever were a real family, I regard as when my childhood definitively ended.

At Mr Rawalpindi's

I haven't managed it, I know. I wanted to tell my story in the hope that I'd understand something – understand my parents, understand us – and in the hope that things would be put in order, put right, laid to rest. But I haven't managed to write even one single episode without it breaking down midway into hypothetical questions and holes, things I don't know and have no way of knowing. Pathetic, isn't it? Even our own stories, we're unequipped and essentially unable to tell.

The writing course ended last night and I realise now, belatedly, how much I'll miss it. Without my noticing, my week has come to be centred around those Monday nights in that dingy, strip-lit room in the Irish Cultural Centre, even when I told myself I was only there for Mr Rawalpindi. The teacher met up with each of us, for a quarter of an hour, to discuss our work. She was kind enough to call it that, to take seriously the sheaves of paper we'd so self-consciously, excruciatingly, slid onto her desk last week.

'I know mine doesn't work,' I said as soon as I went in, to spare her having to say it.

'Why do you say that?' she said.

'Well – it just doesn't, does it? There are too many gaps and contradictions. Too many holes. Too much I don't and never can know.'

She tilted her head to one side and looked at me and I didn't know where to look. 'You have this thing against fiction, don't you, Lara? You think that because you're telling a true story, only the exact and utter truth will do. It's like a moral imperative for you. But, actually, everything we write is a kind of story. We shape it, structure it, decide where it begins and ends. You say that you're stumbling into blanks and gaps and holes – well, what fiction can do is spin a net across them. It won't catch everything – it can't – but what it can do is make you feel what it might have been like, what it would have been like, to live in that situation, to make that decision. Fiction is the most humane and magical of acts – it's healing, restorative, exactly because it shows us a way across those chasms. We can never know what it's like to be someone else, ever, except through fiction. People always talk of fiction as if it's an escape from the world, but it's not that, or not just that. It's an escape out of ourselves and into the world, too.'

There was a lot more, but that was the gist of it. I was hot with embarrassment by then, my head whirling at the thought that she'd actually read my story – parts of it, anyhow – and aching to get out of there.

After I took Mr Rawalpindi home we sat out in his over-grown tangle of a patio garden, all jutting paving stones, rotting leaf mulch and rusting wrought-iron chairs, and smoked some of his weed. It's years since I've smoked, and I remembered why. All it did was make me nauseous, and my head throbbed. Mr R. had dug out some more mouldering boxes, and he showed me the damp soft photographs, brown with spreading water marks and stains. He had his lover's diary, too, an expensive leather journal with gilt-edged pages and tight lines of elegant fountain pen on thick mottling paper. I was there, he said, and he showed me the last few pages where the handwriting faltered, and the entries shortened to indecipherable abbreviations. It was probably more to do with the weed than anything else, and the anticlimactic feeling of finishing the course, but I felt my eyes well up and once they started the waterworks wouldn't stop. I found myself rambling on about how I destroyed our photo albums, and how I didn't ask my mother the right questions in time, and how now all I have of her is her shoeboxes with their useless scraps. Before she died, I'd had the sudden idea of recording our conversations, and I'd bought a stupidly expensive voice-activated digital recorder to leave by her hospital bed, so that if she started talking – and people sometimes do, in their last days and hours – I'd have it saved. But all I got, in the end, was about eleven minutes of my panicked promptings, and her bemusement, and irritability. I've played them again and again, those recordings. I even transcribed them, in case the files were damaged, or lost, or accidentally erased. They tell me nothing, and they're all I have. My mother, stubborn to the end, refused to unburden herself, and my wild hopes that we'd discover a letter, or a diary, something that would explain things or give her version of events, came to nothing.

Mr Rawalpindi listened to me waffling on, and his bright, wrinkled face was so sad for me, so pained, that another bout of tears came out, snotty and gulping. He shuffled off inside and came back with a stained old monogrammed tablecloth for me to wipe my face on, and that made me laugh – wherever does he get such things? – and somehow made things better. It was getting cold by then so we went inside and got horribly drunk on his dusty old half-full bottles of whisky and other spirits that he's somehow accumulated. I sat on a burst velvet armchair that puffed clouds of dust each time I shifted in it, slugged my smeared champagne flute of unidentifiable liqueur and told him everything about my parents and my childhood, the things I'd been attempting to write in my memoirs, the things I'd never confessed to anybody, not even Jeremy. In return, he told me all about his lover, a Waspish New York millionaire who was almost twice his age, who'd whisked him off to New York in the seventies. He'd been saving the story for his memoirs, he said, but was afraid he'd never get around to telling it: he's been writing night and day since the course began and he's still only partway through his childhood. He tried to laugh, make a joke of it, but I had seen the fear ripple through him, and the sadness come down like a shroud. He is an old, ill man, and however he rallies, his body is falling apart around him.

I suddenly sensed how exhausted he was. It was almost midnight by then, and the drink and the weed and the emotions had left me wobbly and drained, too. As I got up to go, he said, 'I think she's right, you know.'

My head was fuggy. 'Sorry?'

'The writing teacher,' he said, impatient. 'I think you should write your story as fiction. Your mother's story. It seems to me that it's her you're trying to reach. Well, write her story.'

'But how would I even start?'

'First of all: by not getting hung up on hunting and pinning down exactly what happened. Like a butterfly collector, you know, those poor dead creatures stretched and skewered to a wooden board. Let yourself be free. Imagine yourself into your mother and write from her perspective, what it was like, being her. When you don't know something' – he tried to snap his fingers – 'like that, just make a decision, use what comes most naturally to fill the gap, and if it doesn't work, replace it with something, until the thing seems to hold together, to ring truest.'

I hesitated for a while, but he was so insistent, I ended up promising I'd give it a go. By the time, then, that I'd helped him empty and clean his colostomy bag – washing and drying around the stoma, reattaching the clamp – tidied up a little and made him a cup of herbal tea, he was drooping in the armchair, almost asleep. I got him into his pyjamas and helped lift him into bed, his body so light and shrunken it could have been made of canvas and balsa wood. I left a lamp on, in case he woke disoriented in the night – he suffers these days, he told me once, from strange, vivid dreams, where the people of his past come back to talk to him – and slipped outside onto the towpath, and home.

I'd expected to wake up able to argue against the promise I'd made. Somehow, though, in the night it had taken root, and the idea of writing as my mother, rather than seeming preposterous, felt suddenly almost intriguing. I phoned in sick to work – the first time I've ever done it, and it isn't quite a lie – and arranged in front of me my mother's things: the transcripts of our conversations, the contents of the shoeboxes. At least, Mr Rawalpindi had said, you don't have to start completely from scratch: some people in the writing group were inventing whole dystopian worlds or alternative sci-fi realities, out of nothing. He's right, I thought. These may be almost nothing, but they are something – the photo negatives, the ticket stubs, the Sylvia Plath with her writing in the margins – and I have my memories, and the little scraps of things she let slip, or very occasionally gave away. It's worth a try, I decided, and as soon as I'd made the decision I was surprised by how excited I felt: daunted, yes, but undeniably excited, too. I have almost a year's worth of holiday saved up, because who takes holiday when you've no one to take it with and nowhere to go? How ironic that suddenly it's a blessing. I'm going to book it off as soon as I can, stock up on basics – coffee, biscuits, wine – and I'm going to start writing, and I'm going to do my damnedest to tell my mother's story.

THE STORY OF JANE MOORHOUSE

Harley Street, September 1971

Her friend Lydia got them the interviews. Lydia's cousin's friend was a receptionist there; that's how word
reached them. The salary, Lydia said, was almost twice
what they were earning at St Bart's, and the hours were
half. It was a no-brainer. They could afford to move
out of their digs and get a nicer flat, in a nicer part of
town. Clothes and shoes and make-up, the lifestyle, all
of it. Snag classier guys, instead of the supercilious junior doctors who thought you should drop your knick-
ers out of gratitude that they'd deigned to pay you the
time of day, and made lewd comments about you afterwards on the ward rounds. Jane was less sure. She was
happy enough at St Bart's: but it was hard to argue with
Lydia's logic, and so she typed up a letter, too, and sent
it along with Lydia's. When she saw the place, she knew
she had no chance. It was right in the middle of Harley Street, steps and columns and gilt-plaque entry-bell,
and inside were thick muffling carpets and art and lilies
in tall vases. The receptionists were like fashion models;
tall, thin, hairdos, faces full of make-up. Lydia had done
her hair in a chignon, and her nails; lots of lipstick, eyeshadow to match the powder-blue skirt-suit she'd borrowed for the occasion. She'd overdone the make-up,
Jane thought, and the skirt was a teeny bit too small for
her, but she looked far more the part than Jane, plain

Jane, with her fawn outfit and forgettable face.

It was a shock to both of them when Jane got offered the job. When you thought about it, though, a nurse had no need for hairdos or mascara. As Lydia said, with the receptionists it was a different matter: they were an advertisement, the first thing you saw. A nurse, on the other hand: well, you wanted your nurse to be neat and clean, didn't you, and that was about the extent of it. Just like Jane: small, neat, anonymous, nondescript. The sort of person that would melt into the background, that wouldn't distract you in the operating theatre. No offence, Lydia said, and Jane said there was none taken. There wasn't, she told herself: she and Lydia were friends, indeed, Lydia was the closest to a best friend she'd ever had. They'd roomed together at nursing college, had come to London together, shared digs together, done most things together for the past three years. It was because of Lydia that Jane had applied for the job, and it was because of Lydia that she took it. Not out of spite: it was more she sensed it would anger Lydia if she didn't.

The clinic had been set up just four years earlier, offering minor facial surgeries. Removal of non-malignant moles, scars or birthmarks; brow-lift, chin-tuck, simple facelift. There were plans to expand – to offer breast reduction and augmentation – but for the moment the surgeries were minor outpatient procedures. The three men who'd established it – an American, an Irishman and an Israeli-born surgeon – had a business model whereby consultants could work private-practice hours at their own discretion, relatively easy and well-remunerated work, whilst retaining their more challenging day jobs. They took out discreet black and white advertisements showing before-and-after pictures in upmarket magazines and the *Times*. Their start-up costs were high, but so were their prices: high enough to reassure. Clients came slowly, at first, but word of mouth spread. Two years after they had opened, they fitted out and equipped a second operating theatre in order to double their capacity. They recruited two more surgeons, of whom Patrick Connolly was one. They advertised for more surgical assistants, the job for which Jane applied. Their permanent employees at the time Jane joined them were two certified registered nurse-anaesthetists, or CRNAs, a receptionist, and four registered nurses and surgical assistants.

She is standing in theatre, holding the tongs that lift the skin of the patient's forehead, while the surgeon snips and extracts strips of subcutaneous tissue and ligates the facial nerves and repositions a slither of muscle fibre. She has been standing for hours – days. She is swaying on her feet, and trying not to sway, and reciting – fiercely, desperately – her times tables. Her surgical mask sucks into her mouth with every shallow breath and she wants to pluck it free, tear it away, but both of her hands are holding the tongs. If she doesn't stop shaking, she might rip the skin of the patient's forehead. Concentrate. Seven sevens are forty-nine, eight sevens are fifty-six. Her own forehead is cold with sweat, and she can feel her gown clinging where her back has sweated. Nine sevens are sixty-three, ten sevens are sev-en-ty. Ridiculous that it should be the times tables. Some nurses recite psalms, or the words of popular songs. It's the times tables that have lodged in her mind but she daren't try to find anything else: and so she clings to them, each conjugation, like rungs on a ladder, like inching up a rope in the school gymnasium, feet clenched, hands burning. It's a mistake, being here. She should have stayed at St Bart's. She hasn't even been here a week, she can't leave. She can leave precisely because she's only been here a week. Oh God, why did she do it in the first place? Don't think now. Eight times one, eight times two, three eights are – Her stomach lurches, but then she has it, twenty-four, and four eights are thirty-two, and five eights are forty and six eights forty-eight. It's working. She's settling back into herself. Her hands are shaking. They are: it's not just her imagination. The surgeon glances at her, his eyes narrowing in the space above his mask. His mask is flecked with blood. Bodily fluids have never made her squeamish before. Seven eights are fifty-six, eight eights are sixty-four.

'Hanging in, there?' he says, his words muffled by his mask, and she nods, not trusting herself to speak, not trusting that words will come out instead of the rush of sour vomit she feels rising in her throat.

Nine eights, nine eights, nine eights. Her mind is losing its grip on the rope. She inches along: sixty-five, sixty-six, sixty-seven, six to seventy and that leaves two, seventy-two. Nine eights are seventy-two. Of course, or eight from eighty.

He swabs and dabs and takes the tongs from her, and her hands fall to her sides, like lumps. When he asks her to hand him the suture kit – proud of his own handiwork, he does his own suturing, where most others leave it to the nurse – her hands are like paws, huge clumsy animal paws that can't pick up or hold or grasp. The other nurse passes the tray with the threaded needle and strips and gauze and iodine swabs. She stands, rushed with heat where a minute ago she was cold. She shouldn't have left St Bart's. She's never felt like this before. She's never been squeamish. At nursing college people fainted every week, for the first few months. For some it was blood, for others slopping out bedpans, or tweezering the packing from a gangrenous sore or infected ulcer. But you got used to it: you got on with it, precisely because there was something to *do*; you kept yourself in motion. Unlike here, where you just have to stand.

The surgeon is finishing up, the CRNA is checking the oxygen mask and the vital signs, the other nurse is replacing the used instruments. Someone has made a joke; they are laughing; she can't keep hold of what has just been said. Ten, twenty, thirty, forty. Tens are too easy. Eleven, twenty-two, thirty-three: elevens, too. It doesn't matter now. It's over. In just a few minutes she's going to leave, and she's never going to come back. She's had it with here, with this place. This isn't even her first procedure, it's her third, and it's got no better. She has to leave. She'll write the letter tonight, give it to them first thing tomorrow morning. Perhaps she won't even have to do that, because this is still her trial period. Perhaps all she'll have to do is tell them – she's not cut out for this – and she can go back to the bustling wards of Bart's and the patients and the cleaning and chatting and soothing and caring. That's what she wants to do: that's what nursing is about, not this. Rich, vain women getting their beauty spots snipped off or their jowls pinned up, this isn't the world in which she wants to spend her life. Much as she and Lydia and the others complained about the junior doctors, at least they were meeting people. Here, it's all women, apart from the fly-by-night surgeons. Fly-by-night: that's like something her mother would say. It's true: they come in, consult, do a procedure, go off to their real lives. None of them stays around any longer than they have to. There's no social life. There's no drinks after work, or cinema parties on the days off, or any of the rest of it. She's never going to meet anyone here.

All of these thoughts are swirling around her head and she starts when the surgeon pulls down his mask and speaks to her.

'You're all right, there?' he says. She realises that it's over: the patient is being wheeled away, the CRNA and the other nurse leaving. It's her job now to clear away the detritus, sterilise the instruments, get the room ready for the cleaners.

'Yes, thank you,' she says, automatically.

'Thought you were going to faint on us there.'

She's flustered by that.

'Ah, I'm only coddin' ya.' He peels off his latex gloves and his hairnet and drops them to the floor. 'You're new here?' he says.

'I started on Monday.'

'How're you finding it?'

'To be honest,' she says, before she has a chance to think, 'I'm not cut out for this.'

His laugh is surprisingly loud. 'Not cut out for it. That's a good one.'

She hadn't intended to make a joke. She's not even sure it was that funny.

'Ah,' he says again, 'that's a good one, I must remember that one. Not cut out for it.'

She's not used to doctors – to consultants – talking to mere nurses. Is he flirting, is he just being friendly?

'I'm being serious,' she says.

'You're a funny wee thing, aren't you?' he says. 'Here, take your mask off, till I get a look at you.'

Flushed, fumbling, she does what he says. She should turn and walk from the room, she thinks. The tone of the way he's speaking to her. Lydia once slapped a lad, or said she did, for giving her lip.

He studies her face. She is nothing much to look at, she thinks. Her face is small, peaky, pale. Neat, anonymous, symmetrical features; thin lips, light eyes. Hair in damp wisps where it's come loose from its bobby grips. A blue vein threaded across her forehead; too prominent; almost ugly. The only feature of distinction in her face.

'What's your name again?' he says.

'Jane.'

'Je-an.' The way he says her name, he splits it in two. 'Je-an what?'

'M-moorhouse. Jane Moorhouse.'

'Well, Je-an Moorhouse' – the *house* like *hice*, like *rice*, like a sneer – 'don't take this the wrong way, but you're going to have to pull up your socks in here, so to speak. If you decide to stay, that is. I understand you're relatively new to this, so I can make allowances. But in the future: there's no room for heads in the clouds. Do I make myself clear?'

It's like being slapped in the face. She doesn't know what to say, or where to look. He claps her on the arm. 'No offence, OK?' he says. 'Just a friendly wee bit of advice.' He turns and leaves, whistling, bundling his gown off and letting it fall behind him, on the dirty spattered floor for her to pick up.

She has never been so humiliated in her entire life.

And this, somehow – perversely, inexplicably – changes everything, turns it all on its head. She won't leave now, she decides that night. She can't. She'll stay, and prove herself. That a man like that can treat her like that: she'll damn well stay, and prove herself. She's stubborn, Jane Moorhouse. Beneath the nondescript exterior, there's steel; there's something stronger than self-pity, something even she doesn't fully grasp or understand, because so far in her unremarkable life she's had no need to. It flexes in her, that night.

The Langham Hotel, 1972

She's been like a virus: crumbs under his skin. He's not used to people being immune to his charm, his banter, his easy good looks. But she is, and it discomfits him. It's nothing he can put his finger on, exactly – she's always perfectly polite; neat and precise and alert. Yet he can't shake the feeling that she's scorning him, or laughing at him, secretly, the whole time. There's some wall he's never encountered before, and when she looks at him it makes him feel watery inside, uneasy, as if she's seeing through to something deeper within. Ridiculous, he knows, to put it in such terms. But that's how it makes him feel. He dreads her being on his rota, and yet he somehow longs for it, too, and one Thursday when it turns out she's back home in Yorkshire it plunges him into a bad mood that pollutes the whole day and evening. She's never the first one – perhaps that's it – to look away. It's always him, glancing sideways or making some excuse to turn away, like a silly, smitten girl. He is at least ten years older than her, and considerably more senior, but none of that gives him the authority with her that it should. He cannot understand it, and it gnaws at him. He thinks about her far more than he should.

His wife is finally pregnant; has a baby, their first. When he's next over in Harley Street he insists on taking everyone out for a drink. The air-headed receptionist, the

CRNAs, the surgical assistant, even the cleaner. Champagne at the Langham Hotel. It's over the top, he knows, but he wants to – what does he want? To provoke her? To impress her? To show his largesse? The others get tipsy and giggly and compete with their cooing over pictures of the baby. She doesn't. He's had fantasies – for weeks, now, he's had fantasies – that when everyone leaves, she can be persuaded to stay, and then— It's awful, he knows, with his wife and four-week wain at home. He knows that. He just can't get her out of his thoughts. She's not – he tells himself – even that pretty. You wouldn't look twice – you wouldn't look once – if she passed you in the street. But there's something about her, there's something between them, and he's damned if he's the only one who feels it. Sometimes he thinks she's playing him. Then he thinks: don't be ridiculous. In the gaps between his visits to London, as he plays things over in his head, her power grows over him, swells and distorts. He has to remind himself she's just a girl. But the thing is: she's not, and he can't explain it.

She stays for a glass and a half at the Langham, choking the sharp-sweet sips of fizz back, then slips away when he's gone to the toilets. Her heart is hammering and her palms sweaty as she hands over the cloakroom ticket. She is angry, furious with herself for feeling this way. It is the moment she realises that she's devoted more time to thinking about him than any of her past boyfriends, or the lads she occasionally goes out with now. None of them have his charisma: they pale beside him, weedy and insubstantial, and she has stopped enjoying – or pretending to herself she enjoys – the cinema dates, the house parties and home-made punch, the desultory fumbles on piles of smelly coats in spare rooms, or alleyways, or when it's her night to have the living-room sofa. She has started to think – she hates herself for thinking it, but somehow doesn't stop it – that he'd know what he was doing. The day she heard, through Jackie at reception, that his wife was having a baby any day now: it was as if someone had punched a hole right through her, and out the other side. She's hated every minute of this ridiculous drink at the Langham. The opulent chandeliered lounge, a second, third bottle of champagne: it's grotesque, inappropriate, more than any of them earns in a week, in two weeks. On the bus home she works herself up into a righteous rage. When she tells the story to her flatmates, Lydia laughs and says, You're completely in love with him. I'm not, she says, taken aback, and Lydia just laughs again. That night, wide awake and miserable, the image flashes into her head: him pinning her down, throwing her around, taking her. This time, she doesn't stop it. God, she thinks, later, smoking one of Lydia's stinking Russian cigarettes out of the bathroom window. I bloody am. She splashes water on her face and vows to redouble her efforts at being cold to him.

A month later, he asks her for a drink after work and she says yes. It's an awful hour and they talk about nothing, the time flies by thinly and then it's over. On the pavement outside the pub she bursts into tears and can't explain it and can't stop it, either. Just shag him, says Lydia. Get it out of your system. The next time he's across in London, there's no drink, no dinner, no pretence. He's consulting that day, no surgery, and after the last client has left she goes into his room, carrying fresh paper covers for the bed. It's the first time they've been alone all day.

'Drink after work?' he says. 'Meet you at the place we went before?'

The door is ajar, and she can hear the receptionists giggling over something.

'Shall we . . .' she says, and swallows.

'Have you been OK,' he says, 'since the last time, I mean? God, when you left like that . . .'

The consulting room is just off the main reception. She glances out. She's got no excuse to be in here. Her heart is pinballing around in her ribcage.

He lowers his voice. 'I haven't stopped thinking about you. Please. Just one drink, that's all I'm asking.'

She's rehearsed the words so many times in her head, over and over at night, and on the bus to work and while she's meant to be doing other things, like listening to her flatmates' stories or Lydia's theories of men, at last weekend's house party while she kissed someone else whose face she didn't recognise even five minutes afterwards. Choosing material for a new dress at Liberty's, material she couldn't quite justify or afford, fingering it and letting herself imagine him unpeeling her from it. In the bath last night, wasting shillings on the meter for the water, and hoping no one asked what she was doing washing and curling her hair on a Wednesday night.

'God, Jane Moorhouse . . .' he says, his voice low and rough, and she can't imagine how she ever found that accent ugly before.

It's wrong. She knows it's wrong, it's utterly, completely wrong.

'Shall we go back to yours?' she says. She doesn't look at him as she says it, and she can feel him start and wonder if he's heard her right.

'I'll meet you at the entrance to Regent's Park,' she says. 'By the Park Square Gardens.'

Then she turns and leaves, quickly, before anything else can be done or undone. Just shag him, lass, and get him out of your system.

'Are you all right?' he says, as he puts the key into the door of his flat. They've barely talked on the journey here – the Tube to Piccadilly, the Tube out west. She's barely been able to look at him as they shared the same pole, bodies swaying, bumping and not-quite-bumping as the carriage jolts and shudders. The warmth, the solidity, the smell of him close. The hand he touched on the small of her back, as she stepped from the carriage at Earls Court. It sent heat racing, pulsing down her spine and in her pelvis. She's blanked all thoughts, all else, from her mind, but them, here, now.

'Jane?'

'Of course,' she says, pretending she's Lydia, Helen, someone who knows what they're doing. Her experience of sex until now has been with fair-haired junior doctors who come within seconds, apologising. Dates who take a whole film to work up to brushing the edge of her breast or thigh, and can't meet her eye when the lights go up.

'We don't have to do this,' he says as they get into the lift.

'Yes, we do,' she finds herself saying, and she looks him straight in the eye for the first time and sees him swallow; the flicker of surprise and then desire in the way he looks back at her. So that's how it works, she thinks, and another rush of heat goes through her.

She is still in her uniform: a simple, white, fitted dress that buttons down the middle. She wishes she could have changed into her newly made halter dress – from a *Vogue* pattern, cut tight at the bodice, and low – but one of the others would have seen and teased her, or asked questions; and if she'd gone home first she might never have found the courage to come back out. He moves towards her. They are standing in the living room of his flat, haven't even made it to the bedroom, haven't even bothered with a coffee, or a tour around. He unbuttons her from the collar down, sinking to his knees as he gets to her waist. He tugs her tights down over her hips and presses his face to her, and she feels her whole body shudder.

They fuck there, on the rug, on the living-room floor. He pulls her on top of him and holds her tightly by the waist as she arches back and moves. Then they're on all fours. Then he flips her over onto her back and raises her legs up, crooks them over his shoulders and bends forward, his whole weight bearing down on her. Again and again he pushes now, urgently inside her. The part of her that loathes herself for what they are doing is gone now and she is desperate for it, for more. She finds herself shouting out, urging him on. Afterwards she feels bruised inside; stinging and tender, torn. She panics and says she has to go. He offers her a shower – coffee – a

144

drink – begging, now – but she says no to all of them. She buttons up her crumpled dress, stuffs on her shoes, tight-less, and leaves. The red haze gone, she is disgusted with herself. That's that, she tells herself. Never again.

She takes the Friday off sick, and the Saturday, so she won't have to see him. He phones: the landlady heaves herself up to the half-landing and yells that there's an Irishman on the phone. She pretends she doesn't hear: knows the landlady is too fat and lazy to come up the final flight of stairs to see if she's in. He phoned, she thinks. He found a way of looking up my address and telephone number and he phoned. Something in her ripples with fear.

What they both thought, then, would be an ending – something finally done, worked out – proves just to tangle and complicate and worsen things more. Something each thought would be sated has in fact been unleashed.

She swore to herself it wouldn't happen again, perhaps even believed herself.

He did, too. Went back to his wife and baby girl and promised himself he'd start again. He'd had affairs before, broken them off before. They'd been desultory, playful flings; essentially meaningless, easy to extricate yourself from. But this – she – is different. He doesn't understand it.

Next time he's in London, it happens again, and then again, and they are having an affair. They tell themselves – and each other – it's strictly physical, as if the physical entangling is less important than the emotional. But soon they are having long dinners, spending hours getting slowly drunk in out-of-the-way pubs. It's spring now, and summer: walks through the rose gardens in Regent's Park, a picnic in Hyde Park, once – even – boating on the Serpentine. One Sunday, they go to the cinema, like a couple, like any Sunday couple. She starts staying over in his flat, the odd night.

When he's away from her, he longs to see her: a longing that's deep and hollow in his gut, stronger and emptier than cravings that can be cured by sex alone. His wife, his child: even when he's with them, she's stronger; even, especially, in absence, in his mind.

In his absence she's stronger than him. She promises herself, each time he leaves for Belfast, that this is the last time. And yet it somehow never is.

The sex is always urgent, as if it is the last time ever, and so they don't take the care that they should. That autumn, she notices the tender breasts and stomach, the secret new semaphored language of strange twinges and sudden dizziness. The first missed period, the urine sample at the doctor's, Miss Moorhouse, I'm afraid the test confirms . . . He's a kindly man, the doctor, with a balding head and milk-bottle-bottom glasses and a slow, precise way of speaking, who offers her his own handkerchief and a chocolate lime from the bowl on his desk. A strange detail to remember, the chocolate lime, but she never forgets it, and she never eats a chocolate lime again; the splintering shards of it, the sickly dry sourness, the way it sticks, undignified, in her teeth as he reaches awkwardly and tries to pat her shoulder: it makes her feel like a child.

146

She tries to explain but it doesn't come out right; she's not crying out of sadness, or not just sadness.

Without thinking it through, she telephones, from a payphone outside the surgery, his hospital, the Royal Victoria on Grosvenor Road, and asks if Mr Connolly could please telephone Miss Moorhouse from the London clinic, he'll know the number, and no, it's not an emergency, although it is rather important, thank you ever so much. She replaces the phone in the cradle trembling, realising too late that when he rings the clinic – rings for *her* – Jackie or Pam will suspect something. Even if he disguises his voice, or pretends to be someone else, they'll know it's him: who else with a broad Ulster accent would be calling the clinic? She panics, then. She'd planned to take the morning off work but rushes back in case he phones. They've been so careful, up to now, in order that no one at work suspects anything. They carry on in public colder to each other than they were when they were really cold. They don't banter – she's come to love that word – and nor does she try and sneak moments alone in his consulting room, as she did in the earliest days. She hasn't let anything slip to any of the other nurses. She's made a point of inventing dates, of telling stories of past dates as if they happened last night. Once or twice she's even gone to the cinema on her own, so that she could report back to them on the plot of the film, and she's used the names of boys she was at primary school with. She's used this tactic with her flatmates, too: pretending it was a one-off thing with Patrick, nothing, a one-night fling. She hasn't fooled Lydia.

Lydia narrows her eyes, and although she says nothing, Jane knows there is a rack of black marks against her for not sharing, not confiding, or seeking advice.

He doesn't phone back: he's cannier than her. She waits by the payphone at the bottom of her street, the rain coming down sideways, and he doesn't ring then, either, not even at their usual time. They have the conversation the following morning in her landlady's living room with its stench of cats and soup and warm urine: a guarded, coded conversation. It feels like an ending.

The sense of an ending continues to build through the next week before he's due over. She feels stupid, wretched. She had let herself wonder, let herself wildly hope. This decides things, then. I've meant everything I've said when I've said I have to be with you. After work she wanders blankly down Regent Street and Oxford Street. There are no Christmas lights this year – the economic climate, the miners' strike – and the streets feel drab and cheerless. It's mild, too, unseasonal. Everything feels wrong. She stops letting herself think what she's thought these last few months, in dark, secret glints; that maybe a baby would force things the other way. She tries not to think of it as a baby, their baby. Sometimes she forces herself to imagine just a seething mass of cells doubling and doubling inside her. An apple pip – a pea – a grape. Not a baby, not their baby. A blackberry clot of swelling, bursting, multiplying cells. Already it's 1.6 cm and will be 2.3 by the time he's over. She looks it up in a book in the library. *Its hands now bend at the wrist, and its feet are already losing their webbed appearance. Its eyelids cover more of its eyes and taste buds are forming on its tongue.* She closes the book, the thick, greasy plastic covers; shoves it back on the shelf. The dry smell of the muffled coughs and carpet dust makes her feel sick. She tells herself it had to end, somehow, some time. She tells herself she's even looking forward, in a dull sort of way, to the termination. She's not strong enough – it seems – to end things by herself, or he's too persuasive, or they mean to and then think: one last time. After this, she'll have the reason – the excuse – not to see him again. After this, they won't be able to carry on the way they have been. Because you couldn't, could you? Knowing it could happen again, knowing that when it came to it, the decision was made the other way. She's been unhappy – not sleeping, losing weight. Mistresses are elusive, and glamorous, and French. She's just a shy, foolish Yorkshire girl. She gets ready to say goodbye to him. One of her flatmates knows of a cottage on the Suffolk coast, a loose relation, or family friend, who lets it out in summertime. There's no central heating, the flatmate warns her, and it's completely tumbledown. She doesn't care. They can't say what they need to say in his flat. There are too many memories there: they need to be away. She arranges to borrow it for the weekend.

She tries her hardest to be rational, practical, to be stern with herself. She shouldn't have got into it in the first place. Though that's no help now. She's being punished. That's no help, either. She's being given a chance to get out of it. That's the best way of looking at things.

But then there are the other times, too. The times when she knows that she wants – more than anything – because it's them – the both of them – and damn the practicalities,

149

and damn the consequences. Lydia – Helen – Jackie and Pam – her parents: they chew through their lives like cows, blinkered carthorses on the plod. She has known extremes of joy and despair beyond any of them, in the last few months. Awoken parts of herself she didn't know existed. Glimpses into what she, Jane Moorhouse, plain Jane mousy Moorhouse, was capable of doing. It fills her with a wild sort of power, this kind of thinking. She knows he feels the same: he says he does. It's more than love, it's need, I need you, Jane.

She lurches from one way of thinking to the other, one certainty cancelling out its opposite. In the endless week before he arrives, she gets thinner and paler than she's ever been, burned up from the inside with the need and fear and desire. She can't be without him. They have to have the baby. How can they have the baby?

Orford, Suffolk, December 1972

The garden of the house is walled, and up the lichened, crumbling bricks climb glossy ivy and a type of clematis which is flowering even now, in December, little puffs of rosy-white petals on stark bare stalks. Pots of winter-blossoming jasmine are placed on either side of the back door, slender dark wands bursting into tiny golden stars of flowers, like a magician's trick caught in action. Once, someone who knew about gardens has loved these plants, chosen and nurtured them, so that there's life and colour even in the depths of midwinter. The garden is unkempt, though, these days; roses that should have been dead-headed frozen and blackened on the stem; a trellis torn in half and bent under the weight of its wisteria. Damp rotting leaves in mounds. Great drifts of tangled grass and weeds on the pathway, moss on the back step two inches thick.

It is morning; not early morning, perhaps ten or so, eleven. They are sitting, not quite touching, drinking oily coffee from chipped-lip mugs on an old tarpaulin they hauled from the shed. The tarpaulin is streaked with oil, clumped with dried mud, dirt. The rugs they are wrapped in smell of damp and dog. She wore, stupidly, a new plum-coloured jumpsuit, sewn from crushed velvet she bought off Portland Place. The hems of the legs are tattered and stained, unsalvageable, and her platforms are caked with mud from the lane. She has given up caring about her clothes. They've hardly slept. All night they held each other and cried and she feels wrung out, turned inside out. The exhaustion and the emotion have made the morning feel strange and new, and she feels light and transparent, as if she's already passed through the worst that could happen, and now she can start again, and anything's possible.

A robin beaks at the hard, black earth. There is a spider's web, perfectly strung from trellis to magnolia tree, the dew-beads on it like the condensed and solidified remnants of a caught dream. That sounds over-done, she thinks, even as she thinks it, but it's what the day is like: it feels overwrought, unreal, and there is a strange lucidity to everything, as if she is taking in more than you normally think and see, in slower motion.

He has just said, What if she moved into his Earls Court flat and had the baby, and they would see what happened then?

She has not yet said anything in return: does not quite trust herself to speak. They went over it, again and again, last night. The conversation, the loops and grooves of it, was no different from the many faltering discussions about the situation they have had over the past few months, each time one or the other of them, but usually her, has tried to end it. He can't leave his wife, not yet. Nicky (she tries to hold herself steady when he talks of 'Cat' and 'Nicky', hating the easy familiarity of it; when she has to refer to them she calls them stiffly, by their full names, Catriona and Veronica Louise) is only just a year old and Cat's had a hard time of it, she hasn't found motherhood easy, it was a difficult birth and she hasn't adjusted. Besides, their families, the church, the marriage. He has a duty to them, she has to understand, and he can't leave yet. When Nicky's a year or so older, when things are different. But for now, he can't, he won't, he's not leaving them.

She should leave, then and there, she knows. If she wasn't so exhausted, she tells herself. If they weren't so isolated in this bloody Suffolk cottage. If, if. There are always excuses. She is learning this now, has learned this over the course of their affair, and says to herself: this is the shape your life will take from here on in if you don't leave now. Half-promises, and endless excuses. Nothing is going to change, she tells herself. If he doesn't leave now, he'll never leave. When Nicky's a year older will become when Nicky's in school, when Nicky's left primary school, when Nicky's left home. If he wants her, if he wants them, he has to do it, now.

'Jane?' he says.

They might be on a stage set, or a film set. The day has that feel to it. An audience, watching, the decision they are going to make.

'Your wife and daughter,' she says, dully, not even bothering to make it into a question. It's not a question: if it ever was, he's answered it now, made clear his choice.

'You know the way things are,' he says. 'I wish I had a different answer. All I can say is . . .'

Leave, Jane, leave, Jane, leave, leave, leave.

There is the distant lap and peal of church bells. A wedding, perhaps. Joyous. They listen to the bells, rising and falling, clamouring. All that they will never have. She

153

turns the mug in her hands. She had thought they would both decide: they'd have the baby and be together, with everything that entailed, or they'd abort it (make yourself say it) and end the affair there and then. It doesn't seem to her that there's another way. And yet what he's saying – except surely he wouldn't, would he?, say what he's just said unless he truly believed that one day, not now, but one day – maybe indeed in a year, or maybe when the baby was born . . . Her dark, secret, sudden hope is that the baby is a boy. He has a daughter. If she could give him a son. All men, don't they?, really want a son. If she could get through the next few months . . .

She's realised that she's allowed the thought of it, of what he's suggesting. Hope is a hardy weed, she thinks, grimly, the hardiest. It would grow in this neglected winter garden. It sprouts up at the slightest, meanest drop of sustenance; it clings, conserves, keeps going. Wrings every possible drop of nutrient from a chance comment, a throwaway remark, something that could be made to mean commitment.

'When you say', she says, 'we'll see what happens . . .'

So many of their conversations are like this: silences, insinuations, things too delicate or devastating to quite be said.

'I don't know, Jane,' he says, and he looks wretched. 'All that I do know is that whatever way my life goes, it can't be without you.'

The church bells ring again, a final burst. Those words, she wants to say, aren't yours to give. You gave them already – on your wedding day – you must have given them and meant them.

'I need,' she tries again. 'I'd need your word. I'd need a promise from you.'

'I promise you, Jane,' he says. 'I promise.' Even as he says it she is aware he's not actually promising anything. It will be, you're not stupid, Jane, a life of half and broken promises.

She has an appointment at the doctor's surgery tomorrow morning, 8 a.m., the earliest they could give her. In order that she didn't and couldn't change her mind, from whatever they decided today. If they are having the baby, this will be her booking appointment: the midwife will take blood samples, weigh her, measure her. If they aren't, then at less than ten weeks, a termination can be booked before the first trimester is out.

By this week, your baby measures about 2½ cm in length and weighs just under 2g. His eyelids have grown to cover his eyes, and fused shut to allow the development of his eyeballs; he will not open them until the 26th week. Tiny earlobes are visible. His wrists are more developed; his ankles have formed and his fingers and toes can be seen. Already he looks more like a tiny human being. His basic physiology is in place.

If she called it Patrick Michael. If she gave it his name.

How would she tell her parents? It was an accident, she could say. A one-night stand. The father was – was a sailor, or an airline pilot, someone it's not possible to contact again. They'll be appalled, but who cares? But is it fair to lie to a child about who its father is? Except she wouldn't, of course: the baby would know its father, and by the time it was old enough for things to matter – how old is that, say, school age? That's five years from now, in five years who knows what will happen? He surely won't still be with Catriona out of duty five long years from now.

She wants this baby, so, so badly. His baby, their baby. So very badly.

'I wish I'd met you earlier, Jane,' he says, as if he's reading her thoughts, 'before. If I'd met you before, none of this would have happened.'

If he'd met her before he met Catriona she'd have still been in school. She doesn't say this. She is used, already, to swallowing back the things like this; ignoring them.

He sighs and turns to pour more coffee. They made it on the stove in an old, Scandinavian-style ceramic pot. They burnt it; it is bitter. She shakes her head.

'I don't know if I should be drinking this.'

He puts the pot down; balances it on a slanting flagstone.

'So what do you think?'

'What do I think, Patrick?' She tries her hardest to sound brisk but she hears the pleading, the weakness in her voice, and a shudder of self-loathing goes through her. Think of how you attracted him in the first place. You mustn't be needy. You mustn't be weak. He despises that. I think I'm going to be sick. She gets to her feet and stumbles out of the rugs towards the wisteria trellis, hands on thighs, bending, tries to breathe. The air tastes like water, sweet and cold. She steadies. His hand is on her back.

'It's all right,' she says. 'It's passed.'

'Have you been . . .' He hesitates. 'Having morning sickness, I mean.' He looks sheepish as he says it: it hadn't occurred to him to ask before.

'No. A sort of dizziness, sometimes. Tiredness. But I haven't been sick.'

'You're lucky.' If he goes on to say, Cat had the auld morning sickness pretty bad, so she did, she will turn and walk away now, out of the gate, down the muddy lane, to the station, and she will close her ears to him if he calls or comes after her and screw it all, screw everything she'll leave behind.

You're always making these resolutions these days, she says to herself.

But he doesn't say any more, just strokes her back, kisses the top of her head.

There is an old birds' nest in the wisteria, a shredded-wheat bundle, tilted sideways. The church bells start to chime: it must be midday, now. They will have to leave soon. They must pack up their things and shut up the house, give the key to the woman down the road, get a taxi to the train station at Wickham Market. The train is at one; there are trains only every couple of hours on Sundays and they have to get back to London so that Patrick can get to the airport for the evening flight home; the one o'clock train is the latest they can leave it.

A patch of wild honesty to her right-hand side, the dirty papery husks peeling back to show the pearlescent ovals within. She automatically reaches out, sliding her fingernail between husk and disc and prising it loose, picking off the seeds. She puts them in her pocket. She'll grow them, back in London, in pots on the windowsill, saving the seeds, year by year, in brown envelopes with the date printed on them.

'What are you doing?' he says.

157

In a stack of paperbacks piled on a chair by the bed, a jumble of detective stories and birdwatching guides bought in bulk from the same charity shop, as the pencilled price in all of them indicates, she found a slim book of poetry. *Winter Trees*, it was called. She picked it out because it seemed the newest, its covers still shiny, though the pages inside were beginning to swell and warp with the damp of the barely used cottage. She read it last night, while Patrick walked into the village to find a phone box and make his nightly call to Belfast. She doesn't read much poetry, but she is taken with these poems, and one in particular. *You will feel an absence presently / Growing beside you like a tree.* She puts the paperback into her overnight case when they leave.

Nothing has changed but everything has. In not making a decision a choice is made. They haven't quite been able to agree, or agreed in time, that they definitely won't have it. He's holding her, now. They're clinging to each other as if they're in free-fall. He's much bigger than her, over six foot, to her five foot two. A bear to her bird. That's part of it, too, of course. He whelms her, physically, as well as everything else. He saturates her sight. When he is in front of her, when he is enveloping her, his big arms and his beard, his broad chest and solid shoulders, she literally cannot see beyond him: there is nothing but him. I would do it all again, I wouldn't trade anything, not even the outcome, not even if I knew the outcome from the start.

Routh, East Riding of Yorkshire, Christmas 1972

The house in Yorkshire is solid, square; whitewashed nineteenth-century bricks. It squats just off the main road, a few hundred yards from the village hall. Jane's mother, as well as the Spratleys who live in the adjacent cottage, and Mrs Dunning from the rectory, hold keys to the hall. A small band of Scouts meets there on Tuesday evenings, although most boys go to Tickton down the road. Church coffee mornings, Harvest Fair. The occasional bring-and-buy sale or parish meeting. This is all there is to Routh. The church and the graveyard, the village hall, the garage, a row of cottages, a few houses and a couple of farms.

Inside, the house is dark. Dark burgundy curtains and wallpaper, dark mahogany table and chairs, north-facing windows that in the winter months let in a damp, sliding sort of light. Jane's bedroom, and Helen's beside hers, are both at the front of the house, looking onto the roads, the fields, the sky. Quilted counterpanes and lavender sachets in the wardrobes. They have lived here all of Jane's life: her father had a bad leg injury during the war – in a training exercise, ignominiously – and has since had a desk job at RAF Leconfield in Beverley. The garden at the back is concreted over, to save the effort of mowing. There is a shed, where he cuts and glues his model aeroplanes: the planes Jane used to love, then pretended an interest in, and later ignored. Behind the shed, pale, nudging clumps of mushrooms grow.

She left it as late as possible coming back here. Patrick had come over for the practice's Christmas lunch, which was hellish – they went to the French restaurant around the corner and all of the time she had to pretend to giggle with the receptionists and the other nurses while the partners quaffed wine and made mock-speeches; then the girls decided to go on out somewhere while the surgeons went to the pub, and she could feel their precious last few hours together frittered away and there was nothing either of them could do about it. She waited shivering outside his flat for half an hour when she managed to get away, but it got too cold and she had to give up and go home, so in the end all they had was a hurried goodbye-and-merry-Christmas in the morning, before he got the Tube back to Heathrow for his flight. It almost undid everything. Then she got back to Routh: and it was the dreariest, dampest day of the year, and her childhood home, the familiar creaks and smells, and she thought, with a dreary sort of despair: no. I've left this behind, now.

The day before Christmas Eve they go for a walk, Jane and Helen. Already, just after lunch (vegetable broth, white margarined bread, wet slices of ham, beakers of orange squash), the day is giving up, closing in; pressed to thin lines on the horizon. They trudge along the main road west to Tickton, single file. They had each, without discussing it, wanted to get out of the oppressive atmosphere of the house – their father's mood swings, their mother's brittle, pleading gaiety – but outside, they find it difficult to talk to each other. A few desultory comments on the weather, on the direction they're headed – and they huddle down into their scarves and duffel coats and walk on. A handful of crows, ragged scraps of soot, wheels against the dull sky; a flock of starlings scatters like torn paper. Beyond the village hall and the cottages, beyond the garage and the few houses, like lone teeth in the landscape, there is nothing but the flat road and fields. They press in to the verge, from time to time, to let a car go by. The mud clumps on their boots until its own weight makes it fall. Their breath raw, snagging in their throats. The fields to each side of them are bare, or else dirty with stubble and stray rotting corn. Occasionally they pass a field with sheep, yellow-toothed and yellow-wigged; old, crafty eyes in thin stupid faces.

It takes about half an hour to reach the inn at Tickton. Inside is a warm, slow fug of bodies and smoke; the spicy, earthy smell of mulling wine; a fire in the hearth. They shoulder their way through the dour locals and the shrieking gaggles of home-for-Christmases, and squeeze in to the bar.

Two mulled wines, Helen has ordered, before Jane has a chance to ask for something else – something non-alcoholic. The barmaid ladles out two sloppy beakers, Helen pays and they push on through to the back room in search of somewhere to sit. Helen sees some girls she knows and goes over to speak to them. Jane hangs back, stirs at the clove-studded orange with her little finger. Tries to look as if she hasn't realised she's on her own.

She is gone too long, and home too little, these days, to keep up old school friendships. She just couldn't move back here, she thinks again. She couldn't. Yet the thought of living in his flat makes her feel sick inside. A sickness deeper than her bones. She dabs the orange slice, bobs it under, watches it swell and disintegrate. She is thirteen weeks, now: far enough along that she could tell people, if she wanted to. The baby is the size of half a banana inside her, and it's physiologically complete: right down to the patterns on its fingertips. Not having it is no longer an option. Luckily, she is not quite showing yet. She is so thin and slight that any extra weight shows up on her, usually, at once: but she's lost so much of late, with Patrick, and everything else, that now she just looks back to normal. For the moment, her trousers still fit, just about, although she has to undo the top button after meals, and her cable-knit jumpers are thick enough to cover her rounding stomach. She's let out the seams of a smart dress for Christmas day, and she'll wear a cardigan over it. She wears her dressing gown over her pyjamas when she goes downstairs, when she's walking from her bedroom to the bathroom, even when she goes to the toilet in the night: but the house is cold – her father doesn't believe in central heating – and so no one comments on it.

A crib in her bedroom? Helen's room a nursery?

She looks over to where Helen is talking and laughing with the girls she knows. She has never felt so alone. The need to telephone Patrick, to speak to him, hear his voice, comes over her so intensely that for a moment she cannot breathe. There is no phone box in Routh, and he can't phone her at her parents' house. Her mother would answer the phone and hear his voice, ask questions – or deliberately not ask questions – until Jane fumbled and caught herself out in some or other lie. They last spoke three days ago, just as she was leaving London, and they won't be able to talk again until after Christmas, when she's back, and he can find an excuse to slip away from his family. There is a telephone behind the bar, she knows. She could pretend it was a wrong number if his wife answered. She could pretend it was a message from the clinic. A New Year appointment rescheduled. An infection. His wife won't know – will she? – that the clinic is shut for the whole fortnight. Of course she'll know. It could be – what could it be? A wrong number is best. She's never rung Patrick's number, but she knows it by heart. She knows because she saw his address on his driving licence and memorised it, and later called Directory Enquiries, heart thudding, and the voice on the other end of the line read it out, bored and efficient, unaware of how significant – how powerful – was that string of numbers. She can't call him. She can't. Imagine if his wife answered the phone and passed it to him, or he picked it up and she was there, and they had to fake a brief wrong-number conversation. He doesn't even know she knows the number. He'd think that something was wrong, that it must be an emergency. It is an emergency! She is pregnant, she is pregnant, they are pregnant. Occasionally, in flashes, it seems preposterous, even to her. Sylvia Plath, again: a poem from *The Colossus*, this time. *I'm a means, I'm a stage, I'm a cow in calf. I've eaten a bag of green apples, boarded the train there's no getting off.*

She's pencilled inside, in her tidy script: Christmas, 1972. The words make her smile, the mixture of wit and fear, bravado. She's learned them by heart and she murmurs them to herself. *Money's new-minted in this fat purse.* It is a comfort to her to think that she has no choice, that things have their own pace now and she's just the vehicle, moved inexorably along, forces beyond her control.

She is going to tell her parents: she has to. But not about Patrick, not yet. She'll just say that she is pregnant, an accident, and she doesn't know the father. The morning she goes, bag already packed, an hour before the train, businesslike. She has rehearsed it in her head, over and over, until it's almost like reading from someone else's typewritten speech. The only thing she got wrong was underestimating how lonely it would feel being back here. Her cold, unlived-in bedroom, her parents, her sister. Christmas.

How would she ever see him, if she did come back until things with his family were resolved? It takes four hours from London to Beverley, if you make the connections, and then on to Tickton – he couldn't come to Routh, her parents wouldn't have him in the house. Would she go to Beverley to meet him? Baby in tow? A night in a boarding house there, a dingy B&B? It wouldn't work, it couldn't. She's always left alone, with these logistics, these worries and fears. When he's there, he somehow sweeps or melts them away, or makes them seem irrelevant. They creep and scuttle back, like rats, the moment he goes, chittering at her in the uncertain darkness.

The twist of sickness tightens inside her.

Then suddenly Helen is there, red-cheeked, breathless,

repeating some gossip she's just heard. Helen is three years younger in calendar terms, light years away in worldliness. Helen drinks like a fish (brandy-and-Babycham, martini-and-lemonade), smokes menthol cigarettes, always has boyfriends on the go. She's at teacher-training college in York but what she really wants to do is start up her own fashion line. Like Jane, she's a dab hand on a sewing machine – their mother taught them both, and they both took to it – and she makes up all the *Vogue* patterns. Today, under her sensible coat and scarf, she's in a scarlet shirtwaister with stiff cuffs and a flouncy bow at the neck. She looks reet good, people say. She always looks great. They are similar enough that you'd know they were sisters, Jane and Helen, but where Jane's features are pinched in her narrow face, Helen's seem to fit, somehow. Jane can't believe the wild, crazy certainty she had that she knew what life was and Helen's was blinkered and dull. How could she think that? Helen has reached the punchline and is doubled over, cackling, grabbing Jane's forearm. Jane makes herself laugh, too. She has no idea what Helen has been saying. All of her – the her that matters – is coiled inwards, around the creel of her son. Their son. She must remember that, she must trust that. Their baby: their son. When she asked the nurse if you could tell the sex of your baby, the nurse said most of the time a mother's intuition was right. Patrick Michael. Patrick Michael Jr. She doesn't like Paddy – nick nack paddywhack, give the dog a bone. He'll always be his full name, Patrick. Patrick Junior. She has to keep faith, and trust, and believe. If she doesn't, she'll go under. She has to remember that certainty she had, the certainty she has, when she is with him.

'Want another?' Helen's glass is almost empty, a couple of centimetres of sediment and a sodden cinnamon stick. She waggles it at Jane, then notices Jane's glass. 'Ey up' – they like to talk Yorkshire to each other, ironically, as both of them are trying to lose their accents – 'you've hardly touched yours, lass. Be a good girl and bezzle it back.'

'Mort sweet for me, this is,' Jane says, trying to play the game.

'A vodka, then? Or a gin? Come on, it's Christmas. And Christ,' she says, dropping the accent and grimacing, 'we've got to get through the evening somehow.'

'I think I'll just have a club soda, actually.'

Helen rolls her eyes and plunges back towards the bar, and when the boy comes around for the glasses Jane pushes the mulled wine towards him along with the empty pints. *Your baby is physiologically complete, now: right down to the patterns on his fingertips.*

They have their second drink. Helen's cheeks flush prettily (where Jane's would come out in blotches) and Jane lets her sister do most of the talking. It's dark when they leave the Inn and start walking back. The wind is raw, and tinged with snow. Their faces feel peeled, their eyes start to weep. Helen links her arm through Jane's and they discuss how awful it is to be stuck at home, how awful it would be to be here permanently. Helen doesn't realise, at first, how quiet Jane has become. When she does, she nags at Jane to tell her.

Jane shakes her head.

166

'Is it a lad?'

'No.'

'It is, and all.' She is silent for a moment, and then she says, 'Is he married?'

Jane gapes at her, then remembers to close her face over. She feels the blood drain from, then flood back to her cheeks: she's grateful for the night, the lack of street lights.

'You wazzock,' Helen says.

They are almost home now, but by unspoken agreement they keep on walking, turn left down Meaux Lane towards the churchyard. All Saints' is a handsome, solemn church, built from sober grey stone; its tower dates back to the twelfth century. Once, people would have walked from hamlets all over for services here. But the last rector left ten years ago and since then there's only been a curate, the vicar from Beverley, who comes twice a month for Sunday Communion and special services and once a month for Evensong. When they were teenagers, Jane and Helen – though mostly Helen – used to meet their friends in the graveyard, practise smoking cigarettes or drinking ginger wine or damson gin that the farmer's daughter used to bring along in battered plastic cartons. They push through the same gap in the hedge now and make their way to the back of the church, to the flat slab of long-weathered gravestone they used to sit on. They perch there now, the creeping chill of it, the mossy damp. Helen lights one last menthol, looks at Jane as she blows out the smoke in a lopsided attempt at a ring.

'You wazzock,' Helen says again. 'You're too naive, Jane. You really are. You're not cut out for that sort of thing. Trust me.' Then she says, 'What's his name?'

'Patrick,' Jane finds herself saying, and it's a rush of relief just to say his name aloud. 'His name's Patrick, and he's a doctor at the clinic – a surgeon. And he's – he's . . .'

How to describe him – where can she possibly begin? He's ten years older than me, and Northern Irish, and six foot three, with wild curly dark hair and a beard and he's the funniest cleverest man I've ever met, and the most maddening, and when we make love he pins my wrists down as if he might break them, and he licks the sweat from where it pools in the small of my back and he laps at me like he could never be satisfied –

'I love him, Helly. I'm head over heels.'

Helen just shakes her head and smokes. Jane hears her words jangling in the air; how cheap and tawdry and meaningless they sound; a handful of loose change. 'It's true,' she says. 'I love him. And he loves me.'

She can tell Helen doesn't know what to say. Helen is embarrassed for her.

'We should be getting back,' Helen says, getting up.

Christmas Eve. Taking cards around to the neighbours, the Spratleys by the village hall, the Dunnings at the rectory, the Sewells and Lamplughs and old Mrs Jewitt. Mince pies and offers of sherry, mince pies and offers of cherry brandy, cups of tea, cups of tea. Down Meaux Lane again to the farm; collecting the turkey; a Christmas pudding exchanged for a joint of gammon. Mixing the stuffing; stuffing the cold, greasy cavity and tying it ready for the morning. Sucking on candied ginger all the while, as a precaution. The fibrous taste of it, sucked to strings in her mouth. Carols on the radio and a fire in the front room. Helen capering and joking about, coaxing smiles from their father. Finding a box of old records on top of her wardrobe and playing, over and over, The Kinks, 'Tired of Waiting for You'. She was sixteen when it came out. The lyrics had just been words, then. They don't have a song. Wondering what he and she danced to, on their wedding day. Knowing she's being childish – knowing thinking like this won't help – not able to help it. The mere fact of being here regresses her; she acts and thinks like a child. If she came back here, she'd get trapped: he'd cease to exist and she'd never leave. Breathe. Christmas Day. Church in the morning, home, peeling potatoes, criss-crossing sprouts, slicing carrots and parsnips to boil, the usual. Sherry, and she allows herself to drink it, sweet and oily, the same bottle as last year and the year before, crusty at the neck; lunch, crackers. It is just the four of them, these days. They'll see their second cousins tomorrow – the second cousins they only ever see on Boxing Day. Their mother's brother emigrated to Australia some years ago. Their father's brother died in Africa in the war. All of their grandparents are passed away, now. It would suffocate her. Her mother, her father, her and a baby. She couldn't do it. Presents are after lunch in the Moorhouse way of doing things. First it's the Queen's speech, everyone gathered round. *My whole family has been deeply touched by the affection you have shown to us when we celebrated our Silver Wedding, and we are especially grateful to the many thousands,* blah blah blah. *One of the great Christian ideals is a happy and lasting marriage between man and wife.* How sick she feels, pinned to the spot. Trying to block it out: it's only words, it's meaningless, it doesn't touch her. *In the United Kingdom we have our own particular sorrows in Northern Ireland and I want to send a special message of sympathy to all those men, women and children who have suffered and endured so much.* She gets up, blurts that she needs the toilet. Her father frowning, her mother blinking and shushing her, Helen's beady eyes. She waits in the hallway until the broadcast is ended. *Christmas is above all a time of new life. A time to look hopefully ahead to a future when the problems which face the world today will be seen in their true perspective.*

Presents: blindly opening, dutifully admiring and thanking. Afterwards, helping her mother with the washing up. The day is almost over. Only tomorrow to get through, then on Tuesday she'll go, the two-forty train. By then she'll have told them; by then it'll be done.

Her mother is washing, she's drying, wiping the soapy smears from the plates and cutlery and handing them to Helen to put away. Suddenly, out of nowhere, her mother says, Are you pregnant? It isn't a question. She stops moving; time slows. Helen is next door, putting the crystal glasses, a wedding present they only use once a year, in their place in the sideboard. Her mother doesn't look at her, just keeps her eyes fixed on the sink, keeps scouring the plates.

'What makes you think that?' she manages.

'I'm your mother,' her mother says, quietly, turning to her now, lifting her dripping hands from their cage of cutlery in a gesture of something.

Her mother is small, bright-eyed, her hair mostly grey,

now, and cut shorter than suits her. Margaret, her name is. Margaret Ann Moorhouse née Pearson.

'You've happened an accident, haven't you? Ah, Jane.'

She is shaking. She is trembling, all over.

'He's married, Mum,' she says. Her script, painstakingly planned and memorised and practised, is instantly forgotten.

Helen comes back into the room: stops. 'Helen,' says their mother, 'will you go and sit with Dad, please?'

Helen looks from her mother to Jane. 'Oh my God,' she says.

'Helen.'

Helen turns and goes.

Jane is expecting her mother to be furious with her, to shout, to rage. She has prepared herself for this. But her mother just stands there and starts to cry, silently, hands forgotten in the nest of knives.

Allenby Mansions, Earls Court,
June 1973

A fortnight before the baby's due, Margaret Ann comes down to London. It's June, and warm, a heatwave rising, but she wears her Sunday-best skirt-suit and matching hat like armour. Nobody in London, on a Tuesday morning in 1973, is wearing a full skirt-suit and stockings, a thick silk blouse and hat and court shoes. Jane will notice the effort, of course, and she hopes her daughter doesn't hate her for it. She should have dressed down, she knows that now, because that would send the message that it wasn't such a big deal. Already she's sweating through the blouse and into the armpits of the jacket, and hoping that if she keeps her arms clamped down it might not show. Her hair is damp, too, under the hat, the hairspray turning sticky; she can feel it. Lipstick melting into the runnels above her lip. She's borrowed a trolley-bag from old Mrs Jewitt and packed it with casseroles, vegetable and meat, and shepherd's pie, all portioned in sealed bags or tinfoiled in freezer-proof dishes. She's been cooking for two days, now, boiling and chopping and frying and baking. There's a cake, too. She feels conspicuous, ridiculous, hauling the bumping trolley-bag behind her, up and down the greasy wooden escalators and airless tunnels of the Underground. Jack gave her money and made her promise to take a taxi, from and to the station, but if she takes the Tube she'll be able to give that little extra to Jane. In the warmth of the Tube carriage, though, she's sure you can smell the food, even through its packaging. The meat, thick and intimate. She didn't freeze it before she came, because it would defrost on the journey, and then you couldn't freeze it again. Her hair itches the nape of her neck and sweat seeps between her breasts and she glances around, furtively, to see if anyone's frowning or sniffing the air. She feels self-conscious and miserable, and this mission feels wrong already.

She's been hoping, hoping and praying, that Jane will change her mind and come back home. Sometimes, she lets herself think it might even be something, having a bantling about the place. The prattle of it, the company, the fat little legs as it learned to toddle. She misses that, the milky smell of them, the way they'd hurtle downstairs as if there was nothing more urgent in the entire world than to give you a kiss. Gone are the days – her days – when a baby outside marriage would be looked at askance, called names, or shunned. There'd be talk, of course, but nothing they couldn't steel themselves against and rise above, and talk always dies down. Jane could get a job, in a year or so; Jack could put in a word for her at the base, or there'd be something in Beverley . . . But Jane has refused even to acknowledge their suggestions. A week ago, Helen phoned to say: Mum, she's not coming home, she's made up her mind. Building her ain gallows and dead set on putting her ain neck in the noose, that's how Jack put it. That was all he had to say about the matter, but it cut him deep, she knows that. It's cut them both deep. You feel your children's pains more deeply than your own, always, even when they're not children any more.

A grandchild. It's just not fair, she thinks, in dark, selfish moments. You're supposed to enjoy every second of it, to be able to boast about it, show the bootees you're knitting and indulge in it all. She hasn't been able to bring herself to knit a single thing, and it was only after a week of sleepless nights that she decided on the cooking and the visit, and there's been no pleasure in it. If only Jane would come back home.

The Tube train rattles and shakes into Earls Court and she tries to blank her mind, to steel herself, for going where she has to go and doing what she has to do next.

Jane has done her best to make the place menseful, as her mother would say, to tidy away the signs of Patrick, his paraphernalia. She did it with a conflicted, resentful heart. The thought of her mother coming makes her feel guilty about being here, even guiltier than she normally feels, guilt she can normally block out. She's learned, the last few weeks, that you just have to keep on, as if you're on a tightrope: not looking around, not seeing yourself from outside or above, just fixing your eyes on a point ahead of you and putting one foot in front of the other and letting nothing else exist. Her mother coming threatens to unbalance everything.

She moved into Patrick's flat a month ago, when her maternity leave started. She quit the job – making out to the other girls that it was a lad from home, and she'd be moving back there – and then she moved to his. It makes sense, she told Helen on the phone. She couldn't stay on in the flat-share with the other girls, not once the baby was born. And what was the point of wasting her meagre

savings and more of Patrick's on renting a room somewhere – provided she could find a landlord who would
have a crying newborn baby – when the flat was there
for the using? Sitting empty most of the time, she said.
And that was true: being in it makes her feel how seldom
he's actually there. She likes his things lying around because it makes her feel that any moment he'll be back,
that he's not gone back to Ireland but only to the corner
shop, or down the road. He's messy, Patrick – no, messy's
too harsh a word, he's just not concerned with fussing,
everything so-and-so. Things rest where they fall, old
newspapers strewn, coffee cups, fag-ends in ashtrays or
saucers. His huge smelly astrakhan, bought at her urging
at a flea market in Notting Hill, that he could never wear
in Belfast and so leaves here, draped over the armchair
because it's too bulky for the wardrobe and too heavy
for the hook on the back of the door. His two scarves
– the one she knitted for him and the silk one that was
a present. They smell of him, and she likes them there,
to touch, to wrap around her neck, or twist up her hair
with. His old-fashioned brogues (nobody wears brown
brogues in London in June 1973, not even men his age
and she loves him for it) by the door and his razor on
the bathtub, his dressing gown on the back of the bedroom door. A stethoscope, a spare packet of cigarettes
and a heavy glass ashtray, a bookmarked book, a medical journal, post stacked up on the mantelpiece, Mr P. M.
Connolly – Mr because he's a surgeon, but sometimes it's
Dr – all of these things are bundled away in cupboards
today, stuffed into wardrobes, behind cabinet doors.
    A small, persistent part of her wants to leave them all

where they are, to challenge her mother. This is my life and this is my choice, so you can swallow it or bugger off back to Routh . . . Life is harder, more complicated, than you can understand, and despite thinking that you do, you don't, you don't understand. It's been hard, her mother's pained tolerance and hurt, her father's deliberate silence. She wishes they'd shout at her, or kick her out, cut her off, and then she could forget about them. A break, clean, clinical, that would be best, that's what she wants. The last time she went back to Routh, two months ago, she was already huge, and her father couldn't meet her eye, and strangely, that was easier. If she could just have nothing to do with them, their judging, their pitying, until he's made the break with his wife and she and he can face the world together, vindicated . . .

So when she finds herself, half an hour before her mother is due to arrive, trying to see it through her mother's eyes for things that might cause offence, trying to have every trace of Patrick neutralised or erased, it's like a betrayal of him.

Margaret Ann clutches the piece of paper in her spare hand, following the directions Jane gave her on the phone. That awful phone call, Jane so flat and distant and final, ordering her to get a pen and paper and reciting the new address and phone number, and afterwards she fell to her knees, kinking, her breath coming in spasms, and it was a good five minutes before she could get up and straighten her blouse and go back to preparing the dinner. She pushes it from her mind as she begins to check off the numbers of the flats. Fifty-four Allenby is a respectable-looking red-brick mansion block, ornate black railings and mosaic steps up to the front door. There are hanging baskets of busy lizzies, purple and pink and red, either side of the entrance, and a shiny brass intercom with individual buttons for each flat. Her bowels are churning, watery. She takes a shaky breath and peers at her face in the distorted gilt reflection, dabs the beads of sweat off her upper lip and thumbs a tendril of hair back under the brim of her hat, then pushes the button for No. 54.

Inside, Jane starts at the buzzer, even though she's expecting it. She goes slowly over to the intercom. The baby kicks at her belly. It's been kicking and wriggling all morning, much more than usual. Perhaps it can feel the nerves, the adrenalin. She strokes at her huge, taut drum of a belly, tries to soothe the baby inside. Patrick Michael, little Patrick Junior, it's him and her against the world, and when he sees his son he'll come to her, he will, she knows he will, she just has to get through this, the next few weeks, days, minutes . . . The buzzer goes again, accusing, discordant, and she takes a breath. Just before pressing it she turns one last time to check there's no trace of him, nothing offensive, nothing her mother can take umbrage at.

But he's here: Margaret Ann can feel him, sense him, even smell him. She stands and stares, taking the whole place in, as Jane busies herself with her jacket and hat. The one wall papered in brown-and-cream fleur-de-lys, the green velour armchair and rust-coloured shagpile rug, the ceramic-tiled gas fireplace. The cabinet of records and the foldaway record player, the lurid yellow poster advertising something called *M*A*S*H*, the framed poem on the wall. *With all its sham, drudgery, and broken dreams, it is still a beautiful world. Be cheerful. Try to be happy.* How dare he? she thinks. Then she wonders if it's Jane's, and her eyes suddenly fill. Don't blink, she tells herself. If she blinks, she'll blub. The place smells male. It reeks of him. Traces of aftershave caught in the soft furnishings, the stale whiff of tobacco. No sign of her daughter, here, but that sad poem. A yellow mackintosh hanging meekly on the back of the door, a hasty pot of blue hyacinths. There's no place for Jane, here. She shouldn't be here. It's wrong, all wrong, all of it. A sour taste rises in her mouth: she swallows it down and coughs to loosen the knot in her chest. Turns away so Jane won't see her face, as if she's taking in the rest of the room. Jane's sewing machine in the corner: her eyes fall on it with relief. Something to comment on; something to say.

'You've settled in, then,' she makes herself say, but from the way Jane's face stiffens she knows that everything she says is going to be taken as an insult, a criticism. She cannot meet her daughter's eye. She bustles – feels herself bustling – into the galley kitchen and starts unloading her tubs and packages. Jane follows, huge, cowlike, behind her, barefoot in a loose orange dress that does nothing for her. Her face is round, girl-like; a big boiled sweet of a face; she's piled on the pounds since Margaret last saw her. You'll never keep him like that, Margaret wants to say. She thinks it with something almost approaching relish, then hates herself for thinking it.

'Meals for at least the first fortnight,' she says, opening the small box of a freezer and packing the food in. 'Chicken casserole and vegetable casserole, you'll see I've them labelled, and those Tupperwares are shepherd's pie. All you'll have to do is take them out the night before and let them thaw, then warm them in the oven, but do take heed you cook them through until they're piping. I've baked a fruitcake, too, in grease paper here; if you keep it in its tin it'll last. That's good for when you're feeding, you'll need to keep your strength up then.'

'Arval bread,' Jane says, a strange smile on her face.

'Beg pardon?'

'Arval bread. Cake for eating at funerals. That's what the old ones call it, in't it? If you'd only see your face.'

Margaret Ann stares at her daughter. She's gone in the head, she thinks. Jane looks back at her with an expression she can't fathom. She has a sudden flash of the girls as toddlers, when you'd caught them at something they knew they shouldn't be doing.

'O Janey won't you think of coming home?' It's out before she can stop herself. 'I own we've been over this and you've made yourself clear but it isn't too late, Janey, it's still not too late. We'll help you, love. We'll redo your room and put a cot in there and when the babby's big enough it can move to Helen's old. You can get a job in Tickton, or Beverley, we can work something out. Oh and don't worry what folks might say, Ann Spratley and the like, they need know no more than we tell them. And wasn't Joan Lamplugh's youngest carrying on with a married man down in Beverley, so it's not as if she'll be able to throw stones anyhow. Please, Janey. Oh, the state of me, look how I'm shaking. I didn't mean to say it like this, but there you go, it's out now. Come back home, love. Come back to us.'

Jane blinks at her, slow-eyed, as if the words are blue-bottles to be brushed vaguely away.

'Would you like a coffee?' her daughter says, excessively polite. 'I'd offer you tea, only I think we're out. And a bite to eat, you must be famished. We've got biscuits, or there's Battenberg, boughten, but it's quite nice.'

The fridge clicks and hums, adjusting itself to its new load. The two of them stand.

She gives way first.

'A coffee would be – would be . . .'

Jane stands aside to let her pass. 'Go on and sit yourself down. You've been travelling, it works you up, I know. I'll bring it through.'

The coffee is aigre and tepid; weak. She turns the cup in her hands, forces herself to sip. She's played her cards too early. Blarting it out like that: stupid, stupid woman. Try again: but how? Which moment to choose, which tone to take?

They sit. Jane doesn't seem to feel the need to talk. She's not even said thank you for the food. She knows that the food wasn't just an offering, but an excuse. Margaret Ann suddenly wonders if *he'll* have the benefit. Sit here forking his way through her shepherd's pie, her casserole. Oh, she hates him. It's strong, this hate, strong and black. God save us. She bites off a hunk of Battenberg, swills her mouth with coffee to swallow down the claggy mass. She tries to think of something to say.

There is a trio of photographs of Jane and a man on

the inside shelf of the glass-doored cabinet: she hasn't noticed it until now. Framed in a cheap frame, the sort you'd buy in the bargain bin at Woolworth's. It's him. Part of her wants to reach for it, to take it out and study it: she's never seen a picture of him before. As soon as she has the thought, another part of her rises up indignant: imagine if it was Jack, and the other woman had pictures of him and her on display. It's wrong, all of it, so horribly, terribly wrong: her daughter is making a catastrophic mistake. She must be made to see, she must.

Margaret gets to her feet abruptly, or as abruptly as she can, and sets down her coffee cup with shaking hands. She can't breathe in here. It's making her sick, being in here, his flat, she can feel it rising again, heaving and greasy, the disgust.

'Does his wife know, yet? And is he planning on telling her?'

Jane blinks at her again, mawky, stupid, and for one pure instant, she hates her daughter, wants to lace her, lam her, hurt her. 'Me and your father didn't raise you to this,' she finds herself saying, and then on and on she goes, everything she's promised not to say, everything she's only thought to herself in the deepest dark of night; it's like a boil, now that she's lanced it, the pus and the poison spewing out, and Jane just sitting there, heaped in the armchair, hands on her huge insolent belly, not saying a word, she should be scringing back in shame but she's not, she's got her martyr-face on and there's nothing Margaret Ann can say to hurt her, she's even maybe enjoying it, the look of her, and this makes things a thousand times worse and somehow goads her into going further than she ever thought of going.

When it's over, the sudden silence between them is ringing. Jane still hasn't said a word: not one flaming word. Margaret's whole body is trembling; she's all iv a atterill, as her own mother might have said: some poisonous vapour gotten into her blood and bones.

'I'm sorry, but it had to be said,' she says.

Jane heaves up and reaches for the coffee cups and cake plates, nests them carefully inside each other on the little round tray.

'Let me take that,' Margaret says. She reaches for it, but Jane holds firm. 'Will you let me take that, dammit.' She might as well not have spoken. She follows Jane into the kitchen. Her legs are shaky beneath her, she's toltering like a sheep with the staggers. Her daughter not saying anything in return is the worst of all.

'Unbethink thissen,' she pleads as she leaves, emotion coarsening her accent. 'Unbethink thissen and come back home.'

When she's gone, Jane opens the freezer and lifts out the first soft package, beginning to crisp at the edges with ice crystals. *Chicken Casserole*, her mother has written in pencilled capitals on a masking-tape strip. She rips it open and lets the contents slide in a congealed heap into the pedal bin. The next one, another *Chicken Casserole*. Another, this time *Mixed Veg*. She opens the first Tupperware, *Shepherd's Pie*, then pauses. It's a fortnight's worth of food, after all, and in this thick June stupor, the heat and the final weeks' sloth, she isn't going to cook and portion food herself, she knows she isn't. Patrick will be over as much as he can to get things ready, but he can't so much as boil an egg himself. The initial surge of cold, pure, intensely satisfying rage is dissipating, slightly. She clicks the lid back down and slides the box back in the freezer and doing so gives her a grim, unexpected satisfaction that she's beaten her mother, after all. She's vanquished her: one more battle won. She ambles into the living room to lie on the rug by the telephone, in case Patrick phones: it takes her too long to get from the bedroom, these days. On the way, she opens cupboards, liberates cigarettes and ashtrays and shoes and scarves. Unbethink thissen, she mocks, aloud. Her voice is thin in the small, dark room. She pictures her mother's lined, pinched, hateful old face. Her accent thickened to almost a parody of itself. Jane tells herself again that she's won. She has. She's got what she wanted: her mum won't come again, and that's what she wanted, isn't it? She's all of a flacker inside, a panicked sparrow in her chest blind-eyed and beating. She eases herself down onto the rug, onto her right-hand side, like the midwife said, closes her eyes and practises her breathing.

Chelsea and Westminster, July 1973

Patrick's there for the birth. Against all the odds, and her sternly dampened expectations: he's there. He's there when the first cramps come, and the seeping waters. There to ring the hospital and ask when to bring her in, there to order the taxi and to push the wheelchair to the ward. There breathing with her, her breath a bubble on top of each contraction, rising as the pain rises. There when the great muscle of her uterus heaves, her body rippling and stretching to ripping point and back again. There when the obstetrician clamps and pulls the baby by the head, draws it out into the world.

It is a difficult labour and his being there is what gets her through. It takes thirty-six hours, and a slit perineum, and feet in stirrups and forceps and haemorrhaging and talk of a transfusion of blood. Even when the gas-and-air wears off, even through the delirium and pain, it keeps her going like a pulse, he's there, he's there, and surely that's a sign.

'Stay with me, Jane,' he keeps on saying, 'stay with me, Jane, stay with me,' and she thinks: now we have to be together.

But the baby isn't the boy she hoped – no, knew – it would be. When they hand it to her, the little grub of a thing, a scrunched-up, boiled-looking face and open wailing mouth, its skull dented and misshapen from the forceps, Congratulations, Mum, and here's your beautiful healthy little girl, she knows there has been a mistake. Congratulations, Sir, the midwife says, as she passes the baby washed and swaddled to Patrick, You're now a father. But he is already, she wants to scream. Even now, she can't give him something he doesn't already have: and the baby not being a boy is a symbol, a message, that things are not going to change.

How could it have gone so wrong? All of them, midwives and friends, everyone she's spoken to, said a woman's intuition is always right. The weight she put on: all the books say that you put on more for a boy than a girl, because boy-babies are generally bigger. The quizzes she did, in library books and magazines: all of them, every time, a boy. She was carrying low, not high. When she craved food, it was salty, not sweet: nuts and crisps, Ryvita crackers with marmite, cheese. Her legs – she's sure this wasn't just her imagination – were hairier than normal, because the testosterone does that. Her pupils dilated when she looked at herself for more than a minute in the mirror – one of her flatmates swore that was a sure-fire way of telling. Even when she did silly things, old wives' things, like adding up the age she was when she conceived (twenty-three) and the age of her partner (thirty-three) and the month in which she conceived (October), it is even, to indicate a boy.

She is incoherent with grief and despair.

'Will you stay?' she gabbles at Patrick, over and over. 'Will you stay even though the baby's not a boy?'

'Shh,' he says, not understanding anything. 'She's

healthy, that's what matters, that's all that ever matters. Of course it doesn't matter that the baby's not a boy.'

It's not just that the baby is a girl, of course: it's confronting the knowledge she's tried to hold at bay for so long, the sheer terror of what will happen next. They try and calm her down. They say it's the exhaustion – the hormones – the drugs – but she is inconsolable and in the end they have to sedate her.

After five days – she's barely out of hospital – he goes back, back to Belfast and on to Donegal, where Catriona and little Veronica Louise are for the summer, with her parents and her brother and his two children and his sister-in-law and her little baby. They're a big clan, Catriona's family. Patrick has used the opportunity of their gathering to come to London and fit in extra consultations: that's been the excuse, and it's not just an excuse, because he needs money, now that he's got a whole new family to support. He's been away too long already – twelve days in total, it's been the longest yet – and he has to go back before they get suspicious, toss wee Nicky in the air and play happy family with Catriona's horde.

The other family: the real family. Jane thinks that she wants to die.

The baby has no name, those first few days. Her name in hospital is Baby Moorhouse, because Jane has gone through all of the appointments under her own name, her maiden name, her only name. She could have called the baby Patricia, she supposes, or Michaela – but these names seem a mockery. For the day or so they have

186

at home, she's simply 'the baby'. In the end, in a panic, amid the fluster of Patrick's leaving for the airport, they settle on Lara, inspired by the *Doctor Zhivago* poster covering up the peeling paint on the back of the bathroom door. But she doesn't have a better suggestion for a name. The baby's sheer physical need for her has stirred something deep, primal; beyond exhaustion or disappointment or any of the usual human emotions. It's as if something in her knows that if she breaks down now, she will be irredeemably broken. So Lara the baby is: Patrick's last, desperate suggestion. Thrown over his shoulder as he changes into a newly dry-cleaned jacket and shirt, and checks the mirror to make sure there's no baby-sick or telltale signs on him. For this reason, he doesn't, says he can't, hold Lara one last time before he goes.

Helen comes to see her: cries at how tiny little Lara is, says how can Patrick abandon them?, that Jane should pack up her things and go back home.

'How are things at home?' Jane asks, and Helen tries to bluff but Jane knows her sister too well and knows she's lying. Their father, Helen finally confesses, is iller than anyone cares to admit. He's always had a temper on him, and in the last couple of years the sisters had put his sudden rages down to fear of retirement, which was imminent, and his gammy leg, which gave him more trouble each winter than the last. 'Ee's a right mardy arse,' they'd say to each other, imitating the accents they were both trying to soften and lose. 'Ee's right radged this morning.' They mimicked him, too, when he stomped out of the house to go to his damp, gluey shed and his beloved model aeroplanes. 'Wert born in a shed, tha gormless lass!' 'Tha's not use nor ornament.' They tried to encourage their mother to laugh, too, as a defence against the ways he'd yell at her. He knew they were laughing at him, and this made things even worse. But now, Helen says, the GP finally convinced him to be seen by a specialist at the hospital, who thought that he was in the grip of dementia. It explained the depression, the violent mood swings, the sudden lashings-out; the way he'd stopped seeing the neighbours or friends, isolating himself in his grey tower of fear and shame. It might explain, Helen says, why he'd refused point-blank to come to London or even to speak to Jane on the phone. It wasn't that he was angry at her, or ashamed, it was just another symptom of the illness.

'If that's any consolation,' she says.

'I can't go back, then,' Jane says, easing the baby from one cracked, swollen nipple to the other. 'Would you go back?'

The fact that Helen hesitates, then struggles to answer, is answer enough.

Another escape route gone. It seems, then, that things can't get any worse. She is trapped, with nowhere to go: trapped in a way she understands she never was before. She exists day-by-day, moment-by-moment: if she thought further ahead, even if it was possible to exist outside the nightmarish present tense of the newborn, she would implode. Something in her switches onto autopilot. The first two weeks, alone, before Patrick can come back: when she thinks back on them, later, she has not a single memory of them.

But things, slowly, start to get better. Helen comes round again, and Lydia, and the elderly lady from 52 calls in twice to clean the flat and make a cup of tea and give the poor new mother a break. She talks about her son, who is in the Army, and Jane realises she assumes that Patrick is too: an army doctor billeted in Northern Ireland. She doesn't correct the old woman, and strangely, the thought gives her strength: there must be lots of wives, she thinks, who have to manage without their husband with them. The wives of soldiers posted abroad, who don't even see their newborn for weeks or even months while they're on tours. She has a way of visualising the situation now, of explaining it to people, of not feeling so completely alone. And she's less alone than she could have been. After that awful initial fortnight's absence, Patrick manages to make it over every single weekend to be with them. More than once she sees tears in his eyes as he whistles and wonders at the difference in Lara, and he says he's dreading the autumn, when it'll be back to fortnightly visits, if that. She doesn't reply when he says that. But she stores the words up and repeats them to herself, turns them over and looks at them, re-plays them, searches them. He's dreading the autumn. He doesn't know how they can do it. That must mean, surely, that something will have to change. To see the way he holds Lara, smiles at her, tickles her feet and blows raspberries on her drum-tight little tummy: she can't believe he loves his other daughter as much. The sickly one, with its allergies, that was colicky and jaundiced and had to be put under a special lamp for UV, and on a special diet. Thinking about it gives her a furtive, guilty sort of pleasure. She and Lara are the family he loves: she sees it in his eyes; she convinces herself she's sure of it.

She starts to pick herself up, to pull herself back together. She goes out walking every single day, for at least five miles, determined to walk the baby weight off. She does it even when she hasn't had a chance to wash her hair and the stitches in her perineum are aching, and she does it despite the difficulties of getting the pram and baby out of the flat. It's Silver Cross, the pram, the latest model, the best that money can buy. Of course it is: it was bought by Patrick Connolly, king of grand, impulsive gestures. It is navy, cot and hood, with two separate clip-on sunshades in broderie anglaise. It has its own lace blanket, too, and two foam mattresses, plastic-lined for protection. But it doesn't fit in the lift: Patrick didn't think of that. So every time she goes up or down, Jane needs to carry the baby in one arm and with the other and her foot tilt the pram up against the side of the lift so that the doors can close. It's a tremendous hassle. If the baby's sleeping, it's guaranteed to wake her up. But she does it, every single day. It wasn't until the baby was born that she realised just how much weight she'd put on: how porridgey her bottom was, her belly, her silver-streaked thighs. She's determined that Patrick mustn't have the slightest reason to leave her. She has sex with him before she's ready, too, reassuring him that it's fine, faking moans and sighs of enjoyment. She remembers what he said

190

about Catriona, how delicate she was, how giving birth damaged her psychologically, which Jane takes to mean she lost the desire for sex. She doesn't let herself wince when the latex of the condom rubs against her dry and tender tissues; she buys an ugly tube of lubricant and keeps it on her nightstand, and she dabs her fingers with it and uses it to lubricate herself so that she's there for him, so that he can't feel the need to turn elsewhere: to Catriona. They don't have sexual relations, he told her recently, and Nicky's almost fourteen months, now: they somehow never started again. She clings to this, yet each day she worries, because of course there's going to come a time when they start making love again, and he's not exactly going to rush to tell her that, is he? Despite all of their differences – in age, in size, in personality – sex has always united them, smoothed over their arguments or tears, reassured them that they're meant to be together, because look at their chemistry, their passion: their bodies know. So she's determined that things must get back to this. It's the one advantage a mistress has, in all the films and books: her sexuality. She doesn't want to be a mistress for ever, but for now, it's all she's got. It's a battle, she tells herself now. She has to make sure she and her daughter win.

When she goes to register the baby, she is forced to leave the sections for the father's details blank, as they are not married and he is not there in person. The clerk reassures her that the missing sections can be filled in by the father easily, at any later date. They will be, she tells him. They never are.

Canada, March 1976

In the spring of 1976, Helen comes down to London to tell her sister that she's emigrating to Canada.

'There's nothing for us here,' she says. 'Nothing.' She gestures at the watery sky, the thin damp grass, the litter and the mud, the blistering rust on the bench, as if she means all of that, too. She can't get a proper job, she goes on, only a couple of days' supply-teaching a week. Her boyfriend, Paul, who trained as an architect, has been unemployed for more than a year, reduced to going round houses offering to do odd jobs, mostly not even for cash. They have no hope of buying a house or starting a family; Helen's dreams of starting up her own business are a joke. So they are leaving. Paul has a cousin who moved to Canada, to Toronto. They are cashing in Paul's small bundle of premium bonds and selling everything they have and they are moving there this summer.

Jane says nothing at first, when Helen announces it. She doesn't trust herself to speak. Helen is the only friend, the closest thing to a confidante, that she has left. She doesn't see Lydia or her former flatmates any more. She can't, for obvious reasons, keep up with the nurses from the Harley Street practice. Her father has had the second of his strokes, and requires her mother's full-time care. She has acquaintances these days – the woman in the post office, the Indian man in the corner shop, the mothers with prams she sees on her daily walk – but she has no friends. She tries to be excited for Helen, or even just a little bit glad. She lets Helen show her the map – the vastness of it. The huge great blues of lakes, and national parks. She lets Helen talk about cabins in the woods in winter, and summers camping on the shores of silver lakes. Skiing and hiking and the cheap price of petrol, the possibilities, the life. You've never been outdoorsy, she thinks, but she doesn't say it. She doesn't say: don't go. Please, please don't go.

'Wow,' she says. It comes out as flat and grey as the day looks, as she feels. 'I mean, seriously,' she tries again, 'that's – that's really exciting. I mean, yeah.'

'It's a much better place to bring up kids, too,' Helen says, and Jane realises she's looking at her meaningfully. She pretends she doesn't notice.

'I suppose it is,' she says, vaguely, and busies herself with wiping Lara's runny nose and tearing off some more pieces of bread – they have come to Holland Park, to feed the ducks.

'Jane,' Helen says. 'Why don't you come, too?'

'Helen,' Jane says.

'But seriously, why not? You could start again over there, you could – no one would know. A whole, new, fresh start.' Jane goes to speak but Helen rushes on. 'You can't carry on the way you're going. You just can't. It isn't sustainable. For you or for her. Think of her, Janey. Think of little Lara. When she gets old enough to ask questions – when she goes to school. When she starts to realise. What's going to happen then?'

'By the time she's in school,' Jane says, stiffly, 'things

will be different.'

'How will they?' Helen explodes. 'You've done this for almost three years, now. God! At first it was when the baby's born. Then it was by the end of the year. Now it's by the time she starts school. He's not going to leave his wife and kid, Jane. He's just not. If he was going to, he would have by now, bloody hell, girl. Don't you see?'

Jane's lips are pressed tightly together. Helen waits for her to speak: she doesn't speak.

'Mum will help you out with the airfare and a bit to get you started,' Helen says.

'Oh, she will, will she?' Jane rounds on her sister.

'Don't be like that. She just wants the best for you, too.'

'So it's all been discussed – decided, has it?'

'No, I just – we just mentioned it, was all. And Mum said—'

'I don't want to hear any more of this.' She shoves the map back into Helen's hand. 'Lara! Come on, sweetie,' she calls. 'The ducks have all had their lunch, now. It's time for us to have ours.' She gets to her feet.

But Helen won't give in: she's been working herself up to this, Jane realises, and is determined to say her piece. 'Please, Jane,' she says, clutching at Jane's raincoat, 'just think about it. You'd have us over there, you'd give Lara a better life, and you get a chance for yourself, too. Meet someone else and start again.'

'I don't want to meet someone else, Helen,' Jane says, shaking her sister off. 'You just don't get that, do you? The thought makes me feel . . .' She tells herself to breathe, not to rise to the bait. She knows, by now, not to try to explain, not to expect sympathy from anyone, not even Helen, maybe most of all not Helen. 'Sometimes, OK?' she says, and it's something she's never admitted to anyone, ever, 'I pray and pray and pray not to love him. To be able to leave him. But I can't. I love him, and I just . . .' She takes another shaky breath. She knows it's no use. She can't even explain it fully to herself. 'I just have to believe, Helen, that one day – because believe me, you're not saying anything I haven't said to myself a thousand times, OK? But I've made my choice. It may not be understandable to you – or from the outside – I get that. But it's my life and I've made my choice.' She bends and hoists her daughter onto her hip. 'We're happy, aren't we, pet?'

Lara wriggles and kicks her muddy little wellingtons against Jane's side; squeals to be put down; stiffens her little body into a plank and reaches for the ducks.

'Mumm-eee,' Lara shrieks.

'I don't know how you do it,' Helen says.

'When you have kids,' Jane begins, but Helen cuts her off. 'I don't mean the having a kid bit. I don't mean the practically being a single parent bit. I just mean – I mean . . .'

The two sisters stare at each other.

'When you talk about – "I just love him" – I mean, God, Janey, you sound like a teenager, do you know that? Do you know how much of a lovesick teenager you sound?'

Jane turns away. It's the last time she ever tries to explain, aloud, to Helen, or anyone, her choices or the reasons for them. She shouldn't have tried, even now. She busies herself with buckling her wriggling toddler into the buggy, snapping the stiff fastenings closed. Finding chocolate buttons to divert the threatening tantrum.

'What's happened to you?' Helen says.

Helen and Paul get married, hastily, at the East Riding
Registry Office in Beverley: it makes their emigration
easier if they are a married couple. Jane doesn't go to
the ceremony. There are old school-friends there, relatives, former neighbours and friends of the family. She
can't quite bear the thought of the scrutiny, the thought of
turning up there with her daughter in tow, and answer-
ing questions about the father or their life in London.
The other reason is that it's Patrick's weekend over: if she
goes back up north, she won't see him for over a month,
and she's scared of this; scared that absence will make the
ties between them weaken, or stretch to snapping point.
For the same reason, she doesn't go to Helen's farewell
party, either. She sees them on the evening before they
fly – their flight is in the morning, from Heathrow, and
so the night before they spend in London and she meets
them for a drink to say goodbye. It is an awkward meeting; Lara grizzling because it's past her bedtime; Helen
and Paul excited and nervous and fidgety, and probably
resentful that she didn't make it to their wedding or their
send-off; nobody saying what they really want to say, or
what they really think.

Alfred Jack Moorhouse
and everything after

She should have gone with them, she knows. It's the new start she needs, and it makes perfect sense. She should have gone with them but she can't. Letters from Helen come, describing their new life, and always ending with: Think about joining us, Janey. The weeks pass, the months pass, and somehow another year's gone by. Lara is three; she'll be starting school next year. Patrick still hasn't left his family in Belfast. Jane's no closer to explaining to herself why she has stayed: why she stays. It's not that she's accepted it: nor even that she's used to it. Perhaps it's that she's gone so far down this road that it seems she can't go back. Her hope, her belief, that one day he'll choose them, is not just delusional: it's not just desperate, either, it's deeper than that. It's necessary. With every day, every week that passes, it becomes more necessary still. She's gone too far, sacrificed too much, not to win him, not to prove the world wrong. She stops asking him, stops trying to manoeuvre the conversation round to it. She just digs in, holds tight, hopes and waits. He loves that she's strong – and so she's strong for him. He loves that she's sexy – so she makes sure that whenever she sees him, she is smooth and buffed and ready, her hair the way he likes it, her make-up, his favourite blush-pink brassiere and cami-knickers. It isn't to diminish their relationship to say that this is surely

a factor, that the honeymoon phase is indefinitely pro-
longed, because they only see each other every other
weekend. Of course now there's a baby, a toddler; smelly
nappies, chickenpox, spattered food and scattered toys,
screaming and tantrums and broken nights. But somehow Jane contrives to ignore this, to minimise it, to concentrate on having Patrick's flat spotless, a cake baked,
his favourite drinks in the cabinet, his daughter in a
pretty dress, herself delighted to see him. She tries not to
cry in front of him, to make him unhappy, to be weak,
or needy: all of the things she's sure Catriona is. She's
terrified that if she lets it slip, even for a minute, she'll
lose him.

He's the only thing she has left. It is as if she is hibern-
ating, waiting. She has retreated almost completely from
the world. She can't let new people in, because then she'll
have to tell them, or else lie to them. The handful of
friends who did visit while she was pregnant and when
the baby was born have slipped away after slowly running out of things to say or ways to be with her, as she
retreats, once she won't listen to their advice which is always, repeatedly, leave him. The estrangement from her
mother is completed, too, because Margaret Ann is able
neither to sanction nor ignore her daughter's life. They
meet, and they have nothing to talk about: no subject is
safe, is uninflected, neutral. Even careful talk of Lara –
how she's growing, walking, then talking – doesn't work,
because the very fact of her is a reminder of the situation. The time between their conversations lengthens,
until it becomes almost impossible to pick up the phone.

Jane sends photographs, now and then, and Margaret Ann sends money; their communications are reduced to this, gestures. Even these are fraught: Jane imagines her mother reads defiance into her sending the photographs, and she sees pity and condescension into her mother's tightly folded wads of five-pound notes. Helen is gone to Toronto. She is completely alone. She falls pregnant with Alfie.

It is intentional. The first time wasn't, but the second definitely is. It is her way of forcing the cards, tipping the scales. Even if the second baby is another girl, it won't matter, because they'll win on the balance of numbers. It's ludicrous, even to contemplate a new baby. The flat is too small, for a start. Money is stretched, even with Patrick's salary, because he's having to earn for two whole lives. It's the only thing, however, that Jane can think of: the only thing she has left. The last three years – *three years* – have worn her out, body and soul, more than she can bear to contemplate. It's all or nothing now, double or quits. She stops taking her birth-control tablets. A part of her feels terrible, it's true: she's like the stereotype of a woman in a magazine, or a villain in a film, trapping the man into having a baby without his knowledge, without his consent. Another part of her, the fantasist, just wants a brother or sister for Lara, wants to be a family. She doesn't have a job, or any degree of independence. She's doing the only thing she can: the only thing she thinks she can.

It's awful with Alfie. She's wretchedly sick, afternoons and evenings. Her skin breaks out in spots; her hair is thin and lank, comes out in clumps on the pillow. She can't help but think she's being punished. She knew Patrick wouldn't be thrilled at the news, but she didn't expect him to take it so badly. Not anger – she was prepared for that, because he's got a temper on him – but quiet, the way he retreats into himself, and she can't get him to engage. She asks him if he'll tell his wife and hopes he'll shout at her, give her a chance to argue her case. Part of her hopes that he'll hit her, drag her by the hair, take control. Instead, he cries. He doesn't want to lose her, he doesn't want to lose Lara, he doesn't know what to do. That's when she realises that she has to take things into her own hands: she has to go to Belfast, and confront Catriona, and decide things once and for all.

*

I've looked at the blank page for almost an hour, now, wondering how, wondering where, to go on. To my surprise, I've come to the conclusion that I don't think I want to, don't think I need to, push on and see my mother in pain, the agonies of it, the guilt, the way it eats her up inside. I'd been looking forward to those parts most: or thought I was. The big confrontation scene, where she tells him she knows his wife's pregnant, and he challenges her, How do you know? Or else breaks down. The scene where we leave, and she waits for him to arrive and see us gone, our things gone too, and doesn't know where or how to reach us. I thought I wanted to write that: to punish him, to see her punishing him, to see them suffering, together, each on their own. I wanted to see how they reconciled: except that I see now that my mother had no choice, or thought she didn't. Even apart from the practicalities and the financial support, need had become a habit, and she didn't know how to live without it. They were yoked together, whether they liked it or not. All the time I watched them as a child, and was convinced that no parents on earth loved each other as much as my mother and father – it wasn't love, it was desperation, and addiction, and a shared guilt, and a need for that guilt and its consequences to feel justified. They needed each other because they had to need each other: because if they didn't, or stopped needing each other, then they were lost and damned. Their need was a force-field, their fantasy, keeping them safe, keeping the world at bay. She wasn't happy, all those years. I see that now. It was shrivelling her up inside, the life she led, the decisions she'd made. Even as a fictional character, I don't want to see her, can't make myself make her, go through all that again. It's taken me completely by surprise, because I thought I was only just starting, getting into the swing of things. But I think I'm done with telling her story now, telling theirs.

There's just one more thing. I've hardly managed to enter my father's head: it's been difficult enough to enter my mother's. But what I have managed, or realised, is this. In Patrick's head, it isn't that he's living one life, in which he's being unfaithful. He's got two lives, and they exist in parallel, separate from each other and distinct, and in and to each he is utterly faithful. The measure of this, the proof, is that he is incapable of ending either. The longer Patrick doesn't leave his wife and child in Belfast, the longer he continues his double lives, the more entrenched, essential, the fact of each of them – the fact of both of them – becomes. You could scoff and say that he's having his cake and eating it. I've been there, many times, much crueller. I don't believe it's as simple as that, though. I don't believe that he enjoys this double life, these double lives, this churning out of lies and half-lies to feed the need of the greater deception. I don't, I really don't. I used to be angry with him, from Fuengirola and for years. More than angry: I used to despise him. Writing this, I realise that really I should pity him: that he ended up living his life like this, split, shackled. It's taken me by surprise, writing that. Instinctively I feel it's true, and something – I'm not quite sure how to put this, except to say that something has somehow melted in me, suddenly; dissolved, or disappeared. I don't need to write them any more.

It's strange how opposed I was to fiction, and for so long. I think it's because my mother and father, I've often thought, lived by stories. They convinced themselves that they were characters in some grand story, some great passion, instead of the reality that it was. Making them into a story, making them into characters in their own story, felt for a long time as if it would be giving in to them. Perhaps it didn't happen like any of that at all. It probably didn't. But I understand how it could have, now that I've tried it.

And I understand too what I need to do next.

WHAT HAPPENED NEXT

Tracking them down

It was easy to find them. Thank God for Google. How, I wonder several times a day, did we ever do anything without it? All I had to do was type in their names and sieve through the results. It might have been harder if either of them had moved from Belfast; but neither of them had. It occurred to me, too, that Veronica might have married and changed her name; but even this problem was sidestepped because she works under her maiden name. Her first name is unusual enough to make it simple to find her; and she's the only Veronica Connolly in the whole of Belfast, so far as I can tell. She is with a practice of solicitors called Cameron Glover, and she's also registered on LinkedIn, so I was able to confirm it was her by the dates and her education. Michael was trickier to find, because there are quite a few Michael Connollys in Belfast. There was the added complication that he could be using his full name, Patrick Michael, or simply Patrick – and there are even more Patrick Connollys in Belfast than Michaels. After a few hours of trawling the results and cross-checking, I was pretty sure that I had him. He was an artist (who'd have thought it? an actual artist, a painter) and he had exhibited in several Belfast cafés and galleries. He taught at the University of Ulster's School of Art and Design, York Street campus, and through their website I was able to find a biography of him, confirming his date of birth, and with a recent photo.

It was strange, seeing my half-sister and half-brother like that. The traces of their lives, radioactive trails; faint but indelible, criss-crossing the internet like flare paths. As I stalked both of them through Solicitors Regulatory Authority web pages, LinkedIn profiles, newspaper reviews, student blogs, Flickr photostreams and all the rest of it, I wondered why I had never done it before, and I didn't have an answer.

So that was that: one afternoon, a couple of Google searches, and I had my half-siblings in touching distance.

It took longer than an afternoon to compose the letter I sent to each of them. That took a full week – not that you'd think it, if you saw the end result. A few sparse lines, saying who I was and how I'd found them, and asking if they would be interested in meeting up, should I ever come to Belfast. I think those short sentences were the most difficult I've ever had to write. I sent Veronica's to her place of work, and Michael's I sent to the gallery that had most recently exhibited his paintings.

It was almost a month before I heard anything.

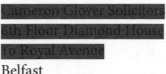

Belfast
Co. Antrim

Friday 22nd July 2011

Dear Ms. Moorhouse,
I am writing in response to your letter dated 5th July
2011. My apologies for the time it has taken me to
reply to the letter, but I must confess that its appearance was unexpected and, I'm sorry to say, most un-
welcome. I do not know what factors may have
prompted you to attempt contact now, after all these
years, and I will be straight with you and say that I
have no desire whatsoever to enter into any form of
correspondence with you or any other members of the
Moorhouse family. I trust you will appreciate and
abide by this. I would further ask you, presuming you
have not done so already, to refrain from making contact with my mother. She remarried subsequent to the
events of 1985, and I feel able to speak for her in saying that any communications akin to the letter you
sent to me would prove most distressing to her.

I thank you for your time and understanding.

Sincerely,

Veronica Connolly

From: Michael Connolly <Michael_connolly@me.com>
To: Lara Moorhouse <laramoorhouse@yahoo.com>
Sent: Wednesday, 27 July 2011, 22:19
Subject: your letter

Dear Lara,

Jeez. It was a surprise to get your letter. It took a while to reach me because the gallerist you sent it to was away on summer hols and the gallery was closed over the Twelfth weekend. But got to me it did eventually and I must say I didn't exactly know what to think when I opened it. A whole welter of thoughts and emotions if I'm honest. I have often wondered what happened to you and your brother. You ask in the letter if I would be prepared to meet up, should you ever come to Belfast. Well, I think the answer is that yes, I would be. Do you have imminent plans to visit or was the situation hypothetical?

Best wishes,

Michael

Patrick Michael Connolly

I met him on a Friday evening. I'd flown into Belfast the night before, and spent the day wandering the city. It wasn't at all what I expected. It wasn't what I'd remembered, under a miasma of slow, stupefied grief. If you don't know Belfast, if all you know of it is the litany of murders and maimings, the annual images of marching and rioting, the hardened male voices defending or accusing on the radio, there's nothing to prepare you for how beautiful it is. True, it's not beautiful in the way Dublin is – squares and parks and elegant Georgian buildings – or with the variety of London, or in the sultry way of a city like Paris. But it's beautiful nonetheless, lying low against the lough, nestled on all other sides by hills. Belfast is a city cupped, cradled in the palm of a hand; a broken creature, something precious. Walking through the streets that morning, I was struck when I realised that at the end of every road, even in the very centre of town, you can see the hills, purple with heather, rising up ahead, so close it feels like you could squint and touch them. There was a neatness, too; a modesty in the city I wasn't expecting. You think of it as harsh and male; defiant. Those voices again: salty, gravelled with ingrained distrust. But the streets are tidy, many of them newly paved, with tubs of bright flowers and young slim trees, and the people are all too willing to nod hello or point you in the right direction. I walked all around the wide streets of the city centre and the square of the City Hall, and out to the University and the Botanical Gardens, then back down to the Waterfront where I sat on a bench in the salt-fresh breeze and remembered and wondered. I had a lovely day for it: that helped. Clear and bright; warm enough to not need a jacket. Only a few fleecy clouds high in the sky; the light full and almost liquid, as if you could breathe it in.

Strange, as I walked those streets, and the streets too around the budget hotel where I was staying, buzzing with cafés and bars and glass-fronted design studios: from time to time a brief, fierce stab of something would hit me. Something I can't put a name to, even now. Not envy, or regret, nothing so simple as that. It was something, perhaps, akin to acknowledgement of the years and the waste that it took to get this far.

He was already there when I arrived, a deliberate, excruciating five minutes late: the John Hewitt pub on Donegall Street. He'd got a table in a far corner, and he was facing the door, a pint of Guinness in front of him. The pub was pretty full, even that early in the evening, but you couldn't miss him: he was obviously looking for someone, scanning the faces of everyone who walked in. I saw him, and I saw him seeing me, all in the same moment.

I'd rehearsed the moment so much in my head, anticipated it so. When it actually happened, as it was happening, it seemed to pass too thinly, inconsequential.

He half got up; waved me over. I excused my way through a knot of people at the bar.

'A'right,' he said, 'how's about ye?' Casual as anything. And I may as well say it now: apologies for the clumsy way I try to render his accent on the page. 'You must be Lara, I'm Michael, pleased to meet ya.'

'Pleased to meet you too,' I managed.

'What are you drinking? I thought of gettin' ya a Guinness, or a half, but I didn't know if you'd be up for that?'

'No, that'd be . . .' I said, not wanting to disappoint already. My voice sounded apologetic; English, weak.

'Come on, I'm only coddin', what would you rather?'

'Actually, I'd love a glass of white wine. Thank you.'

'No problemo. All right – hang on a sec.'

We did a funny sideways sort of dance-jiggle as he shuffled past me and I leaned back to let him pass, so that neither of us would touch. He went up to the bar. God, I was grateful for the breather. It was throwing me off, him being so casual, so friendly. As if we were just two acquaintances meeting, not two people who'd lived the majority of their lives in each other's shadow. I sat on a stool angled so I could see him, and watched his back at the bar; his profile when he turned to joke with a woman standing next to him. I'd seen pictures of him online, of course, but that was nothing to seeing him in the flesh. He was tall, good-looking – in a ravaged sort of way. His face was pale and unshaven – two or three days of stubble, glinting gingery-black. He looked older than his age. He looked like an artist, too: at least in what he was wearing. There was a sort of carelessness to his clothes: beige chinos, rolled up unevenly at the bottom, white plimsolls, a sky-blue linen shirt, creased, unbuttoned at the neck. I immediately felt overdressed and ever so boring, in my sensible cream blouse and Whistles sale skirt and court shoes. I'd felt so smart in the hotel room. I'd even put on lipstick.

Don't be silly, I tried to tell myself. This isn't a date. But it was a date, of sorts.

I tugged my blouse loose from the waistband of the skirt; mussed my hair a bit. I even undid a button before realising that it might look like I was trying to seduce him, and fumbled to do it back up again in time. Blotted a bit of my lipstick away. My stupid, boxy handbag: fake designer, so shiny. I should have come as myself.

He came back with my white wine and slid into his seat, and for a moment or so we studied each other's faces.

'We don't look like each other,' he said.

'No,' I said. Even apart from the style of clothes, we didn't. He had my father's hair, dark and wild and curly. But his eyes – bright blue – must have been his mother's. His way of looking at you sideways out of them. His build, too, he must have got that from his mother's side. He was tall, as I've said, but slim, almost thin; sloping shoulders that hunched in on themselves; cheekbones. Whereas I – but you know what I look like. I wondered if Veronica looked like him; a version of him. In the thumbnails I'd found online – on her solicitors' website – she looked vague, stern, bland. Hair scraped back; steel-rimmed glasses.

'Well,' he said, and he said some unpronounceable Irish word, raised his glass and took a steady swallow.

I took a gulp of wine. Never has a drink been so welcome.

'So,' he said. 'Here we are.'

I took a breath, and tried to straighten out my swirling thoughts, and launched into the speech I'd prepared about how good it was to meet him, and I was sorry if I'd offended his sister by writing to her, and all the rest of it.

His face clouded over slightly when I mentioned his sister. I stopped, worried I'd said something wrong.

'I've never been big with Nicky,' he said. 'She's – how do I put this? – she can be very pass-remarkable, if you get my drift.'

'Oh,' I fumbled, not knowing what to say. Then I said, stupidly, 'That's a good word, pass-remarkable.'

He looked at me as if I was insane.

'Are you close with yours?' he said, after a moment. 'Your brother, I mean.' He looked away, as if his question was only casual. But he hadn't been quick enough.

'When we were children,' I began. Then I thought of Alfie's life these days, thought of mine. The Christmases and family dinners they suffered me through, his daughters with their stifled giggles and bribes if they'd stay in the room and talk to Auntie Lara. 'To be honest: not really,' I found myself saying. I always tell myself that but for Danielle, my brother and I would be close, but perhaps it's not true, after all. I hadn't realised it until I said it.

'So he's not interested in – all this, all this meeting-up malarkey, then?'

'I don't think so. In actual fact, I didn't even tell him I was coming. So I suppose there's your answer to the previous question. We can't be that close at all, can we? I did tell him I was writing to you, and to – to Veronica. And

he wasn't too keen on that. He didn't think it was . . .'
I tried to remember the word Alfie had used. 'Sensible.
Sleeping dogs, sort of thing. So . . .' I shrugged; ran out of
steam. Took another too-large too-fast mouthful of wine.

'Well, Nicky's always been the sensible one of the two
of us. So if your brother's the sensible one of youse –
I guess that makes us the crazy ones.' He flashed me a
nervous grin: it *was* nervous, and I saw that for all of his
charm, his casual greeting, his act of being at ease, he
wasn't, either.

'You're not – married, kids, sort of thing?' he said.

'No,' I said.

'Me either. Nicky is. Girl and a boy.'

'Alfie the same. Only he's got two girls. Twins.'

'Nicky's a solicitor.'

'I know.'

'Of course you do. What's your brother do?'

'Estate agent.'

'House in the suburbs and garden and dog?'

'Yes. Well, apart from the dog. But they do have a cat.'

'You and me really are the odd ones out, then. The
misfits.' He looked at me intently. 'We're the misfits,' he
said again, and then laughed before I'd had a chance to
think up something witty or reassuring to say. 'We're the
broken biscuits. Here, is that a line from somewhere, dja
know? Or am I making it up? Hang on, I think I'm—
D'you know the Pulp song?' and he suddenly sang a few
words. '"Mis-shapes, mistakes, misfits." There you go. I
was right all along.'

Once more, I didn't know what I was meant to say. To
buy time, I reached for my wine glass, took a swallow. His

mind was too quicksilver for me.

'I'm sorry,' I said. 'It's probably an anticlimax for you, meeting me.'

He looked immediately disappointed: you could see it, rippling through his face.

'I'm not what you expected,' he said.

'Oh, no,' I said, horrified. 'I don't mean that at all, I meant – I really did – I meant *me*.'

The next few minutes are a bit of a blur. It felt – I remember this feeling – as if something was slipping through my hands, a rope made of water I was trying to clutch but which just kept pouring away. The pub was really filling up, too, which made it hard to hear each other. Somehow – I have no idea how – we persisted. Things settled again; lost the feeling of lurching irretrievably out of control. We talked a bit about Belfast, and my trip over. How surprised I was at how pretty, how intimate, how friendly the city was. We finished our drinks and I went up to get us another.

The alcohol began to do its work, then, with those second drinks. We started to talk about ourselves – ask tentative questions about the other. Our day-to-day lives. I won't try to write it all down; so much of it was banal, meaningless in and of itself. It was only the fact of it being the two of us there, saying those things, that made them important.

We talked about London, his painting. He'd often thought of moving to London, he said. Then he laughed. He had a quick laugh that came often; a lopsided grin. He'd often thought of moving to Buenos Aires, or Ulan Bator. He might as well. He had no real ties here, a bit of teaching at the art college, an occasional evening class, nothing you'd call a real tie. No wife – no children.

It was the second time he'd brought up wife and children.

'You've never' – I hesitated – 'met anyone? Or . . . ?'

'Ach, there's been a couple,' he said. 'I can't say there hasn't been a few. Truth be told, I'm a bit of a bastard, really. I sort of – lose interest, you know? I'm not actually that nice to them. Woe betide anyone who tries to tell me that, though. So, in answer to your question: nope. I'm a lost cause.' He smiled. 'Yourself?'

I told him, briefly, about Jeremy. I told him about the new blonde – wife, now, I realised, it wouldn't be girl-friend any more. I told him about the baby; how I'd been included in the round-robin email with the picture, the screwed-up mewling little face in a babygro with ears like a rabbit. I told him how it felt to see that baby, his baby, whether he'd meant me to see it or not; whether it was a kindness – before I heard it from anyone else – or a mistake, hitting 'send to all', or if his life had changed so much it hadn't even occurred to him what I might feel on seeing it.

'Bastard,' he said. 'What a fucker.' He was only saying it dutifully, of course – what else could he say? But for some reason, I found myself telling him about the Danish clin-ics, the idea of a baby. I might still do it, I said. I don't think I will, but I might. When I'd finished, he just looked at me for a while, and then when he did say something all he said was, Well, fair play to ye. Fair play to ye. And yet it felt – there's no way of putting this sufficiently – as if the almightiest burden had been lifted from me. I don't even need to do it, I thought. But I can – I could.

It was silly, I see now. It was reckless: the alcohol, the nerves. But at the same time, it felt like something, it really felt like something.

We had a third drink; a couple of packets of crisps. We went outside to smoke a cigarette – he smoked Marlboro Reds, full-strength, and I cadged two of them, although I hadn't smoked in years. The conversation stuttered and flowed, coming up against unexpected obstacles, and finding unexpected ways through. How surreal it feels now, writing it all down. But how necessary somehow to fix it, to have it, to pin it down and preserve it.

'Dja know Louis MacNeice?' he said at one point.

'No,' I admitted, wishing I did. 'Is he – a friend of yours, another artist, or . . . ?'

'Nah, nah. He's a poet.'

'Oh. Sorry.'

'No, sure, why would you know him, you've no reason to. Born here, lived most of his life in London. Died, late sixties, I think it was? Somethin' like that. "When I was five the black dreams came, nothing after was quite the same." That's him. "I peel and portion a tangerine and spit the pips and feel the drunkenness of things being various." That's a great line there, is it not, "the drunkenness of things being various".'

'Y-yes.'

'That's what he's most famous for. But my favourite is . . .' He closed his eyes and leaned his elbows on the table, touching the tips of his fingers chapel-like together, and began to recite, '"The rain of London pimples the ebony streets with white, and the neon-lamps of London stain the canals of night, and the park becomes a jungle in the alchemy of night."'

He opened his eyes and grinned at me. 'Powerful stuff. I did my degree show on those lines. "My wishes turn to violent horses black as coal, the randy mares of fancy, the stallions of the soul, eager to take the fences that fence about my soul." Isn't that great, that. "Eager to take the fences that fence about my soul." What is it, Christ, near fifteen-odd years ago. They've been coming back to me lately, those lines. Been thinking I might – I don't know. Do something with them. Fences of the soul. You know?'

He laughed.

'You think I'm talking out my hole.'

'I don't, honestly. Honestly I don't.'

'Aye, you do. Maybe it is all bullshit, after all. But what can you do?'

'I don't,' I said again. And then, before I could think about it twice and decide not to say it: 'I'd love to see some of your work, your paintings and that.'

'You would, aye?'

'Yes. I – I'd love to.'

'Ach, sure.' He thought for a moment, tipping his head to one side and gazing at me, bright-eyed, ironic, sizing me up. It was the sort of directness that's beyond mere intimacy; a directness that forgets to be conscious of itself.

I felt the heat rising to my face. Always, since I was a little girl, my neck and ears have flooded red when I'm embarrassed, pools that collect in my cheeks and are slow to disperse. I felt the rush of it now, and I couldn't think of where to look or what to say.

'Sorry,' he said abruptly, leaning back and sending his

stool screeching across the floor. 'Terrible habit of mine. Would you for once have some manners Patrick Michael, the ma always said, and stop gawping at people.'

'It's all right,' I said, after a moment. 'You're an artist. You look at people – it's what you do.'

He grinned at me. I found myself grinning back, and pretty soon both of us were laughing – laughing hard, laughing at nothing.

'Come on, then,' he said, when the last wave of laughter had subsided. 'Too nice a day to be in here anyways.'

He picked up his pint and drained the rest of it, holding his mouth open to let the lacy beige dregs slide in. I gulped the last mouthful of my wine.

'Right,' he said, setting his glass down and slapping his palms on the table. 'Are we off, then?'

'We are.'

'It's not too far.' He looked dubiously at my shoes. 'Are you able?'

My feet, swollen in their stupid shiny court shoes, were throbbing already. But of course I didn't tell him this.

'Well, as I say, it's just a wee dander. And it's not a night to be indoors.'

He was right: it wasn't. The sky outside was a deep, deep blue. There wasn't a cloud to be seen. The sun, surprisingly strong, was slanting golden. The streets were filling with people, spilling from bars and pubs, smoking and drinking and laughing and calling greetings to passers-by. Their ties loosened or removed; their jackets slung over shoulders or on the backs of chairs. The pavements exhaling the warmth of the day; high up, hundreds of starling-flecks whirling and tumbling. Music cascading from bars. A Motown hit here, there some Van Morrison. I caught a snatch of the Shangri-Las, some Beyoncé. There was a carnival feel to the evening, I thought. It felt like a film set – as if everything had been chosen and placed, as if everyone was the most perfect version of themselves. It was the sort of evening that felt as if anything could happen, or perhaps already had. When there is an alignment between all of the parallel worlds spiralling with every instant, every decision, away from this one, so that all the people you could have been and all the choices you could have made, all of them, for a moment, touch. That sounds too much: reading that now, I'm cringing at myself. But that was how it felt: that sky, the sun, that Belfast night. Once again, I thought, incredulous: I hadn't known – who could? – that it would be so beautiful. I felt – and it wasn't just the warmth of the drink – lit up inside.

'Skeepinup,' he called over his shoulder, or something to that effect.

I nodded vaguely, then realised he was still looking at me, watching for my response.

'Mmm,' I tried. He looked amused. 'Sorry,' I said, 'I love your accent, it's just . . .'

'You could strip paint with my accent,' he said. 'Stop being so polite. If ever you don't catch me, just say, Whoa, Mikey – Well go on, say it – go on!'

'"Whoa, Mikey",' I said, conscious of how ridiculously round my vowels sounded. Conscious that it was the first time I'd spoken his name, out loud, to him.

'That's better!' he said. 'What I'm just after saying is, it's keeping up. The weather. It's holding for you.'

'Oh! Yes, it seems to be.'

'You're lucky. You never get days like this in Belfast. Not in September. Fuck, not in July or August either. Dja know they sell holidays here to Egyptian women, based on the premise the soft Irish rain'll do wonders for their complexions? If it doesn't rain at least fifty per cent of the time they get a full refund.'

'Is that true?'

'Would I lie to you?' He laughed. 'Who knows? Sounds like a good idea, anyways. If they don't already do it they should.'

We shouldered and wove our way down a tiny cobbled alley, hung on either side with huge, drooping hanging baskets and crammed, absolutely crammed, with people.

'Duke of York's,' he shouted. 'They do good live music on a Thursday, if you're ever back.' We fought our way through and turned right into a bigger street and he pointed out bars as we walked. The Black Box, it was a good music venue, too; the Spaniard . . . Down there was the Merchant Hotel, but of course I knew it, didn't I, because I'd said I was staying at the Premier Travel Inn opposite. Well, a couple of streets that way was the River Lagan, that direction was the Waterfront Hall, five-ten minutes that way was St George's Market, it was good on a Saturday, they had loads of farmers'-market-type stalls, a decent fishmonger's, cakes and craft stalls, sort of thing, different bands each week . . . I should go there tomorrow morning, if I had time. I should go here . . . I should go there . . . Had I seen that? . . .

Several times he paused in his tour-guiding to nod or raise a hand to a friend or acquaintance across the street.

'It's so – friendly,' I said. 'And all of this – I mean – wow. You know? Just – wow.'

I must have sounded – something; envious, or wistful, because he hesitated for a second; glanced at me. 'None of this would have been here ten years ago,' he said. 'This wouldn't have been the Belfast Dad knew.'

'No,' I said. 'I know.'

'This isn't the place we grew up, either. Nicky and me. Well, it is and it isn't, know what I mean? Sort of almost makes me think sometimes – I don't know why I'm saying this to you – that you can change, you know? I mean I don't mean you, I mean – "one". Anyone can.'

All traces of the joker had fallen away from him as he said that. His mouth, his eyes, were completely serious. Without the wisecracks, he looked older; sadder. In that moment, I loved him. I felt it: my heart swelling, actually swelling, warm in my chest.

'I never used to think it was possible,' I said. 'But you're right, maybe it is.'

I'd said too much: been too English, too earnest. Perhaps anything I'd said would have been too much, whatever way I'd said it. His face resumed its ironic expression.

'Listen to the hack of me,' he said. 'Leopard like me doesn't change its spots, I'm tellin' ya.'

He lit another cigarette, without offering me one. We walked on.

A couple of side streets, a couple of minutes more, and we were at his studio. 'Been here near ten years,' he said, as he felt in his pocket for his keys. 'Gonna have to move on soon, I reckon. Landlord wants to put the rents up.

Or else sell it.'

'I'm sorry.'

He shrugged. 'Everythin' changes. Isn't that what we're just after sayin'?'

He seemed angry, suddenly. I didn't know why: if it was something I'd said, or if there was something I wasn't saying that I should. His moods, I was realising, were mercurial. One minute he'd turn the full warmth of his sun on you, the next it was shadows. That's Dad, I thought, and I remembered how as a little girl I'd do anything to please him, and how my heart leapt when I won a smile from him, a wink or a ruffle of the hair, or the prize – how ridiculous, how pathetic it sounds now – of a 'wee Squrl'.

We climbed four flights of concrete stairs, the stairwell dingy and the painted railing peeling in places, or rusted where it was peeled completely bare. He climbed fast, two steps at a time. I followed as best I could, my feet burning. By the time we reached the top it felt like a knot was tied behind each of my knees.

'We'll just have a wee gleek in,' he said. 'Don't feel you have to, I don't know. Think of something to say, or anything. My work's not for everyone.'

I was wishing now I hadn't come. There was nothing I could say, I thought, that would be the right thing. I tried to catch my breath, lengthen and still it.

He opened the heavy door into his studio.

I followed him in, and temporarily lost all thoughts of everything.

It was white, his studio: high-ceilinged and flooded with light. There were windows on three sides, the view from the right the glittering river, from the left the city, ending in those ever-present mountains. Cave Hill, Carrick Hill, Divis, the Black Mountain – I'd looked up the names in my guidebook – were purple and black and grey against the gathering sun. I turned, slowly, taking it all in. Maybe I'd be an artist, I thought, rashly, impulsive, if I lived and painted here.

'You like it?' he said, and his voice was light and amused again.

'I love it,' I said. 'Oh—'

'Hold your horses, woman. You haven't even seen my paintings yet.'

'I'm taking my time. I'm – acclimatising. I've never been anywhere like this before.'

I tore my attention from the windows and took in the studio itself. The floor thick with spattered paint, the four, five easels set up in different places, with paintings in various stages of completion. The canvases stacked four, five deep along the back wall. Paintbrushes in mugs and jars of water. Half-finished mugs of tea, a kettle on the ground plugged into the wall. A couple of half-eaten sandwiches. A stack of Jaffa Cake boxes. An empty bottle of wine; a half-full bottle of Bushmills. Saucers used as ashtrays, full of cigarette butts; their faintly dry, stale smell. The clean smell of turpentine, or white spirit, whatever it is artists use to clean their brushes. The oily smell of paint. The light, the space. I'd never been anywhere like it before.

'I'd've give it a lickinapromise if I'd know we'd be coming back here,' he said, nudging aside a mug with his toe. 'I tell a lie: it's always piggin.'

'It's wonderful,' I said. 'And it's all yours. Oh' – suddenly remembering what he'd said about the landlord, and the rents. 'I'm sorry. I forgot, I didn't think . . .'

He shrugged. 'S'what happens, isn't it? You have to move on. You can't rely on anything being permanent. And I've been here donkeys – never expected it'd be this long. Just the way it is. Fresh pastures.' Then in an American accent: 'Fresh kills.'

I couldn't tell if he was being sarcastic or not. He didn't seem angry, though, so I moved to an easel to look at one of his paintings. To tell the truth, I wasn't sure what it was, or what it was meant to be. It was huge swirls and swoops and blocks of colour, scarlets and oranges and golden and greens. There was another, similar, on another easel, but this one was in blues and blacks and yellows and streaks of crimson. The paint was put on thickly, so that in some places it was crested in peaks. Other parts looked like a comb or a stick had been dragged through them, and you could see other colours breaking through from underneath.

'They're – powerful,' I managed, shyly. They were. You could feel the energy from them, pulsing.

'They're cityscapes,' he said. 'These here are more figurative.' He gestured over to one of a woman, lying naked on a sofa. She had brick-red hair, mussed up, that fell halfway down her back. There was another of the same girl, a close-up of her face this time, and another of her neck and bare shoulders. I'm not very good at describing art. But again, looking at them, you felt a sort of energy: an angry energy, this time. They were raw, incredibly sexy. Almost too intimate to be looking at. In the full-length one she had pubic hair, unwaxed or trimmed, like a snarl of orange wire wool. One finger was dipped in it, coiled. She was staring back at the artist as he painted her with an odd sort of expression: provocative, but almost, if this is possible, at the same time pleading.

'That's Catherine,' he said. 'Or Katya, as she likes to be known.'

'Is she – I mean, was she . . . ?'

'She's a postgrad student of mine. I told you I was a bastard. This is Anna.' He dragged out a canvas from the wall, another naked woman, painted from behind. 'And this' – a Spanish-looking girl, painted in black outlines and block colours – 'is Miriam. This is Miri, too.'

The last one was a view of the inside of a woman's thighs, seen from just above, as if you were kneeling, her knees held open by just-seen hands.

'Right,' I said. 'They're . . .' I tried to find a word that was complimentary, and not – what was the word he'd said his sister was? – *pass-remarkable*. 'Interesting,' I finished, lamely. But he didn't seem to hear.

'I tell myself it's because I'm an artist. We have different needs to normal people. Different rules apply. But basically, I'm just a cunt. A bit like my Da.'

Neither of us said anything. The sun was setting now, throwing all sorts of shadows on us inside. After a minute, he restacked Miriam and Anna.

'Well,' he said, and he spread his hands in front of him, palms up, in a mocking, ironic sort of way. 'Now you've seen my soul.'

'We have the same hands,' I said. We did: I'd noticed in the pub, when he was quoting poetry, and I did again now. We both had our father's hands, long and slim with tapering fingers.

He laughed, and it wasn't a nice laugh.

'I was always so jealous of you,' he said quickly, not meeting my eye. 'You and your brother – Alfie.' He pronounced the name at a distance, with care.

It's the sort of cliché the writing tutor would say not to touch with a bargepole, but you could have knocked me down with a feather. I think my jaw actually dropped and I gaped at him.

'You were—'

'Jealous of you, of course, madly. You were obviously the ones he wanted. We weren't enough for him. Otherwise – Well. Why would he have done it? I bet if he could've divorced my ma he would've. I always used to think he was probably waiting until I was in secondary school, you know, the way some folks do. I mean it can't have been fun for him, can it? No, you were his real family. The ones he wanted.' He spoke fast, but quietly.

'Michael,' I said. 'Michael . . .'

There weren't the words. Even if I'd been the sort of person that was good with words, I doubt there'd have been the words.

'But Michael,' I said again.

He met my eye for the first time since he'd begun his speech; forced a laugh. 'It's OK,' he said. 'I mean it's not as if I'm bitter or anything. Ha. Not that that sounds – What I mean to say is, I've had long enough to get over it, haven't I? Or at least I should have done.'

He turned away, walked a few steps towards the Lagan-facing window. Neither of us said anything for a while. The sun was almost fully set, little more than smears of red and orange on the river.

'He was a weak man,' I said, slowly, and as I said it I realised I'd never put it in those terms before, so simple, so human. 'I always thought – and I mean right up until this year, I thought – that he was some kind of heroic figure, like a god or something, you know, from a legend. That he loved on a different scale, a different plane than normal people. Than the likes of me. But now I – meeting you, and hearing – everything you've just said – it's just dawned on me. That, well, yeah. He was a weak man, not a strong one. He wasn't some Byron, or some Casanova. It's the opposite. He was a slave to – he let himself be ruled by – his lust, and his – and when you look at the trail of, you know, devastation he left behind? It isn't that he'd rather be with you, or with us. It's that – he was too greedy, too weak, and' – I couldn't believe I was only just realising this, there, now – 'he didn't have a superhuman love, after all. Not at all. God, I think that's the longest speech I've ever made.'

It was: I think I've managed to capture it down pretty much as I said it, as it falteringly, stumblingly, but irrevocably occurred to me.

He walked past me and stooped down, a darker shadow than the shadows; picked up the Bushmills bottle. He uncapped it and swigged, then offered it to me.

'No, thank you,' I said reflexively. And then: 'Actually, please.'

He handed me the bottle, his hands – our hands – shaking. I took it; glugged, the firewater fuming and scorching my throat. Wiped the lip, and passed it back.

He twisted the cap back on it, and set it down.

'What are you doing for the rest of the night?' he said.

'What? Oh – nothing, I mean – I have no fixed plans.'

'Shall we go kaileyin'?'

'Shall we go *what*? I mean' – and I tried to imitate his accent, the way he'd said it earlier – '"Whoa, Mikey".'

It was a lame excuse but the excuse to laugh has never come as such a relief.

'Kaileyin', he said. 'Like – shall we go out on the lash? Make a night of it. Paint the town red.'

'I think I'm a bit old for that.'

'So'm I. But it's never stopped me yet.'

'All right, then,' I said. 'I'd like that.'

'Right y'are, then.' He paused. 'What you just said about – our father.'

He stopped. *Our father* hung in the air.

'What you just said about our father. There's a couple of lines – here, hang on a sec.' He flicked on a light – the shock of it, like being plunged into cold water – and went over to a stack of books in a corner and squatted down beside them, rifling through. 'Here we go.' He motioned me over and stood up to show me. It was a battered green and cream paperback, a pencilled portrait on the front, stuffed with Post-its and coloured tags, its margins full of scrawled notes.

'It's my MacNeice, from college. My *Selected*. Here. Page . . . seventy-one, here we go.' He cleared his throat. 'It's the one I was quoting at ya earlier, about London. There's a verse in that – this here – that makes me think of Dad.' He cleared his throat again. '"Under God we can reckon on pardon when we fall, but if we are under

229

No-God nothing will matter at all, arson and rape and murder must count for nothing at all."'

It was utterly still in that room, as he read. Everything – even the sunset – seemed to have been stopped, for us, to hear those words.

"'So reinforced by logic"', he read on, his voice growing louder, "'as having nothing to lose, my lust goes riding horseback to ravish where I choose, to burgle all the turrets of beauty as I choose."'

He stopped, closed the book. 'Well, that's what I think, anyways. Here. I think you should have this.' He held it out.

'Me? Oh, no, I couldn't – not your personal copy, with all of your notes in it. Thank you. But—'

'Lara,' he said, and the way he said my name wasn't like the stripping of paint, but softer, like gravel through water. 'Lara, I'd like you to have it. It's been – good, you know, meeting you. Good for me. I think it has. And I'd never have had the courage to look you up myself. Write to ya out of the blue and that. Go all the way over to see you.'

'Well,' I said, and I took the book he was still thrusting at me, smoothed its cracked cover and ran my thumb over its dog-eared corners. 'Thank you. Thank you for this, which I shall treasure, and thank you for – well, for agreeing to meet with me, for a start. For allowing me to see your wonderful studio, for—' I stopped. 'I've actually – that is – I've got something that I thought – that I thought I might . . .' My mouth has never been drier. I pulled the sheaf of papers from my handbag, crumpled from where I'd folded and stuffed them in. 'I thought I might give this to you, and then I decided of course I wouldn't, but then, after what you said, about me and Alfie being the family that – which is so not true – I don't know, feel free to throw this away, or whatever, but if you were interested even a little bit in hearing my side of the story – I've done my best to get it down.'

'You're a writer?' he said, taking the pages.

'Oh God, no, no, not at all. I went to some classes – but only because I was taking this old man, a patient, well, a friend, actually, who wanted to write down his life story, you see. That's sort of how all this started.'

He flipped through the pages.

'Please don't,' I said, 'not now. It's – it's not literature, I'm not a writer. It was just a story I had to tell. On every single page of it I was excruciatingly conscious of how much I wasn't a writer. The way your poet – MacNeice – captures London in the rain in just a few words. I could never do that. The people, the places – they're not even a ghost, here, of the real thing. But maybe you'll read it, and . . . Well. You'll understand, or at least understand a bit better.'

'My turn to say thank you,' he said.

Another moment, and something seemed to pass between us: something asked – or answered – agreed.

'Right, well,' he said. 'We're in danger of getting dead heavy, here. I hope it's not just me that could do with another drink.'

'I'd love another drink. And a bite to eat. God, I'm suddenly starving.'

'Come on, then.'

He was right when he'd said 'misfits'. We were: both of

is, in our own ways. But for the briefest of moments that night, our jagged edges fitted together and made each of us more of a whole.

My brother and I left his studio and descended into the Belfast night.

From: Michael Connolly <michael_connolly@me.com>
To: Lara Moorhouse <laramoorhouse@yahoo.com>
Sent: Sunday, 18 September 2011, 23.12
Subject: your story

Dear Lara

Well, I read the manuscript you gave me over the w'end.
I'm not sure what I expected. But whatever I expected,
that certainly wasn't it. You said you're no writer, and
certainly it was raw in places (not that that's a bad thing,
necessarily) but I found it extremely moving, and I don't
think that's just because of my personal involvement in the
story. I'd never thought how hard it must have been for
you. For your mum. Jesus.

You've an ear for the way people talk, you know. I think
you must get that from our father. He used to be involved
in a lot of amateur dramatic productions (that's how he
met my mother) and he was able to take off anyone, my
uncles and aunt always say of him he'd have everyone in
stitches. Anyhow, that's by the by. You should consider,
and I really think this, doing a course or something, maybe
an Open University one or a correspondence one that
would fit around your schedule, that you could do in your
own time. Have you ever thought about that? To be fair
I'm no real judge, but I wouldn't say it if I didn't think it. I
think you've got something there.

On another note: I'm having a show this November, at the
Mullan Gallery on the Lisburn Road. I don't know if I
mentioned it? If you were interested, or wanted an excuse

for another visit, you should come over. The opening night is Friday 18th, and my mother and perhaps my sister will be there then, so for your own sake that probably wouldn't be the day for you to come. (Though I told them I'd met up with you: there's been too many secrets in this family. Nicky's face though I say it myself was a picture.) But it'll run until Christmas, so any weekend after that – or indeed during the week if that suits better. I'd be happy to drive you round, take you to a few more places. You'll no doubt see Belfast in its natural state, i.e. cold and wet and windy, but what can you do.

Glad to hear you're liking the MacNeice.

Think about an OU course.

M.

AFTERWARDS

It's over a year later now, as I write this. Many things have changed, since I wrote those last pages, my account of going back to Belfast. Most in ways I would never have predicted, could never have imagined.

Mr Rawalpindi died. That's the first thing I should say. It happened fast: within a few days. He didn't, in the end, as he'd dreaded, have to go into a nursing home, lose his dignity, his independence. I returned from Belfast and found out he'd collapsed at home a day or so before; the interim carer found him and he was taken by ambulance to hospital. It wasn't anything specific, or new, just his whole body packing in, organ by organ. He died in Hammersmith Hospital on Monday 19th September 2011, and I was there, though he was unconscious and had no way of knowing. I miss him every day: almost as much as I miss my mother. Another person I lost, and realised I'd lost too late. I wouldn't have any of this, wouldn't have done any of it, if it wasn't for him.

I'm still writing. Writing more than ever, in fact. At Michael's suggestion, and with the encouragement of the teacher at the Irish Cultural Centre, I'm enrolled on a course with the Open University. The strange thing is, though, that when it came to deciding what I was going to write, I realised I wasn't going to write my story or my family's, after all. I thought about it. Thought about giving us all voices, or even telling it from my father's point of view. But it seemed, finally, that there was no need to. I've told that story: I'm at peace with it now. That's not to downplay how important the telling of it was. Writing my story, I think, in many ways saved my life. It certainly changed everything: the course of bitterness and recrimination and despair that I fear I was set upon. It let me forgive my mother, and let go of my father. It let me meet my half-brother, and in a small way, help him too to let the past go. I've been over to Belfast twice in the past year, and we email each other occasionally, and it helps to know that we've got each other. Writing this gave me a purpose, too, a goal; a reason to get up in the mornings. It taught me that writing isn't self-expression, vomiting self-pity onto the page. It's the taking and shaping of things, carefully, again and again, until they make a sort of sense that not only you but others can understand, and maybe benefit from. At the start of this narrative I'm obsessed with *knowing*. I've come to realise that you can never know: but you can understand, and that's what fiction does, or tries to do. It takes a detail – one of the myriad details that are or could be true – and burnishes it until it is somehow more and better than itself, and in the light of it you can start to understand: just maybe, perhaps, in a little way, what it's like to be someone else. I'd never, for a start – in fact until Michael said it – considered how hard things had been for my mother. She was in love. For better or worse, she loved my father.

If only I could have realised that when she was dying: realised that what I needed to say wasn't How could you?

or even I forgive you, but just I understand. Our conversations then were circular and fragmented and frustrating, me desperately trying to wring from her any facts, or scraps, that she could possibly remember. She was wary of my Dictaphone, and thought I was trying to trap, or to punish her; to force some kind of deathbed confession. Perhaps I was, and I regret it: regret not just letting her lie, and holding her hand, stroking the side of her face, and saying, It's OK, it's OK, as if I was the mother then and she the child.

The story I'm writing now is Mr Rawalpindi's story. It's a story that needs to be told, and he'd be so thrilled if he knew it was going to be. His life in Anguilla, the most northerly of the Leeward Islands, and his childhood in the Valley, and around the cays. Seal Island and Dog Island, Prickly Pear Cays. Learning to swim before he could walk; fishing with his father and his brothers. Spiny lobster and crab; conch and mahi-mahi, red snapper, shrimp. His parents' story, as he gleaned it, and as he told it to me: their lives as indentured Asian Indians, brought to Guyana as teenagers in 1915, and moving after the war and emancipation to Anguilla; getting married; their smallholding, and the living they scraped from the thin, dry soil. The goat, tethered to a post at the back of the outhouse. The pumpkin patch, and the three rows of tomato vines; the patch of leafy green callaloo. The stakes for pigeon-peas, and the pepper-plants. The mounds of cantaloupe, and the lime tree. The rattles and bowls they carved from gourds, to sell to white people in the market. The necklaces made of dyed pumpkin seeds that he and his brothers made for the youngest sisters. All of this, I'll try to conjure up. His decision to migrate to Britain in 1957, aged twenty-one, having heard the reports from Jamaica and the *Windrush*. How he never imagined that he'd never see home again. His life here, his realisation that he was gay, and the first man who broke his heart. The wealthy old New Yorker who fell in love with him and flew him across the Atlantic, and whom he nursed through a stroke and the pneumonia that eventually killed him. How does a poor immigrant West Indian meet and bewitch an old, white Rothschild? I'll try to make it real, to get under the skin of things. Then the bequest – the return to London – the house in Hammersmith – the lovers of his later years. All of these stories I'm going to tell, all of these stories that make up him, and his story, and I'm going to do my best to do it all justice.

There's been a further unexpected outcome from writing my story. The teacher at the Irish Cultural Centre runs some workshops for troubled teenagers, and suggested I might get involved – they're always looking for volunteers. Metres of red tape and multiple CRB checks later, I started in the New Year, and I'm now working towards a Diploma in Caring for Children and Young People. And that's not all. I'm about to move in with Jake Obigwe, one of the youth workers on the scheme. He's five years younger than me; unmarried; no children. I know that's true because I've met his mother. His mother, and his sister (his father died when he was ten, so we have that together), and goodness knows how many of his cousins and aunts, and godchildren galore who adore him. God knows what he sees in me. I'm not, after all, exactly what you'd term a catch. But there you go. Life – love – is at once the most mysterious and the simplest thing in the world. If there's hope for me, there's hope for anyone. It may be too late for children of our own – I'm turning forty now, after all, and besides, we're only just moving in together; it's a big step from that to babies. But both Jake's mother and his sister are long-term foster carers for the Borough of Hammersmith and Fulham, and for the first time it occurs to me that this is something I could do: that we could do, because you don't need to be rich to do it, or even married. The children you love don't have to be your own. And God knows there's enough of them in need of a little bit of love. Mr Rawalpindi, I think often these days, must have loved me like a daughter, although I was too blind to see it at the time, and thought it was me doing him favours. I want to give someone the chance to be loved like that. I know I have it in me, love and what it means to love, the capacity for it: I never knew before.

We'll see. Reading back on that, I'm sounding like a giddy teenager. I don't care! The short of it is that there's hope, now, avenues opening in all directions, where before it seemed there was nothing. I look back on my opening pages now, and think: I began with the utter devastation of a toxic nuclear landscape. How much more obvious can you get? How damaged I was; how scorched and ruined. Yet I didn't for a second see it at the time. If it was fiction, I doubt I could get away with it. I could change it now, could take it out. I'm about to give my pages to Jake for him to read: he's been plaguing me ever since we met to let him see what I've been working on, and now that we'll be living together, I'll have to let him in. I can't say I'm not nervous – I'm terrified, in fact – but I'm taking consolation from the fact that he's such a slow reader, it'll be at least a year before he gets to these pages, and if things haven't worked out then, I can quietly remove them from the sheaf before he ever realises he was almost part of my story.

But something in me, some small, fizzy, hopeful part, doubts that'll be necessary.

Who knows? Who, two years ago, at the start of this, would ever have dreamed of any of it?

There's something I need to do first, though, before I hand over these pages. I have this idea of my mother, on a spring morning in 1972, in an attic room in the house she rents, getting ready to meet her lover. I've been thinking of it in unguarded moments, her, there, poised on the edge of everything; young and happy and hopeful. Hopeful that it will all work out somehow, because she's young and it's a clear blue day and she's in love. That should be part of this story, too.

There's a phrase she used to use, when Alfie or I wanted something we couldn't have. Beggars can't be choosers, she'd say. If wishes were horses, beggars would ride. It's an old Yorkshire saying, I think: something her mother used to say to her. It's coming to mind, now, as I write these last words. As if all my wishes have come true, in ways I could never have expected, let alone dared hope for. Glossy black stallions, their muscles rippling beneath their skin, their manes and tails astream. And riding on each, a tattered-cloaked beggar, wild-eyed and barefoot

and exuberant, taking all the fences that once fenced
them in with an exhilarating, breakneck, devil-may-care
speed.

L.M., London,
February 2013

Appendix: transcripts

INTERVIEW NO. 1

Date: 2.2.10
Time: 4.25 p.m.
Place: Isabel Hospice, Welwyn Garden City
Subject: Jane Moorhouse

Q. OK, so just to recap, I'm turning it on now. OK.
   It's . . . twenty-five past four on the afternoon
   of Tuesday 2nd February. Um . . . OK. We were talk-
   ing about – do you remember? – on Sunday after-
   noon. We were talking about – Do you remember the
   cat he bought us that time?
[Two-second pause]
Q. The white kitten?
J. What is this?
Q. We talked about this. On Sunday, remember? We
   agreed we were going to do this.
J. I don't know what you're bothering me for.
Q. We talked about this.
J. I don't know what you're talking about. Stop mitherin'
   me. Why are you trying to . . .
[Three-second pause]
J. You're trying to trap me, aren't you? Trap me with my
   own words.

Q. Calm down, Mum, I didn't mean to—
J. She's trying to trap me. My own daughter. Well you're not going to catch me! I'll tell you that much, Madam, I'll tell you that much for nowt.
[Six-second pause]
Q. I just wanted to ask you about the white kitten.
[Ten-second pause]
J. You can wait of me all you like.
[Twenty-second pause]
Q. Mum? Are you still awake?
[Recording ends.]

INTERVIEW NO. 2

Date: 5.2.10
Time: 8 p.m.
Place: Isabel Hospice, Welwyn Garden City
Subject: Jane Moorhouse

Q. That's it on now, so I'll just leave it there and . . . Hang on . . . Yeah no, it's on, so . . . Just . . . Leave it there and, while we chat, OK? Oh, wait a minute – it's eight o'clock p.m., well, just after, on Friday 5th February. So . . .
J. [Incoherent]
Q. What's that, Mum?
J. [Incoherent; coughing]
Q. Do you want some water? Hang on – here you go. Do you want me to . . .
[Sounds of rustling; pillows being arranged]

Q. Is that enough, there, or do you want – do you want me to – Are you OK, now?

J. Stop mithering me, love, I'm fine.

Q. OK. OK.

[Three-second pause]

Q. So I thought we'd – I mean – I just thought it would be nice to—

J. Why are you recording it?

Q. Why am I recording it? We talked about this, Mum – I just – didn't we? – thought that, well that – you know, if it was recorded, or, or written down or whatever, because – don't you? – you forget. And there's so much that—

J. [Incoherent]

Q. What's that, Mum?

J. What do you want to know?

Q. What do I want to – well – I guess – Well, what I guess is – what I suppose – I suppose I was just thinking about when you and Dad met, you know, and . . .

[Ten-second pause]

Q. Well, I mean . . .

[Three-second pause]

Q. I mean if you don't—

J. Thursday 14th September 1971.

Q. Pardon, Mum? What's that?

J. The day I met him. Thursday 14th September 1971.

Q. Oh right. Really? I mean – you remember the date?

[Two-second pause]

J. Of course I do, love.

Q. OK, right, but . . .

[Six-second pause]

J. I'm tired, Lara.

Q. I know, Mum, of course you are, of course, but –
Thursday 14th September 1971?

J. That's the day. [Coughing]

Q. You're OK, Mum, you're OK – here – let me . . .

[The pouring of water, the rustling of pillow
and bedclothes]

Q. There you go. Are you OK? You're OK now.

[Two-second pause]

Q. So if you could just – I mean just if there
was anything . . .

[Six-second pause]

Q. OK, how about this. How about – what about this,
Mum? – how about I just talk, sort of remember one
of my memories, and you – well, you sort of, I don't
know, if there's anything you want to say, to add or
whatever . . .

[Two-second pause]

Q. OK, so does that sound . . .

J. I'm tired, Lara.

Q. I know you are . . . I won't – tell you what, just five
more minutes, OK? Just five minutes – I'll time it,
here, look, I'll time it here and . . . Right, so, the other
day, OK, when I came to see you on Tuesday afternoon, we were talking about the cat. The white kitten,
remember? Do you remember it was one of Dad's
Thursday presents? I think I would have been seven
or something, six or seven – or actually maybe it was
even earlier? Five would you say? No I couldn't have
been five. Six, say. And Alfie, what does that make

Alfie, still just a toddler? – and Dad brought home the kitten, in this sort of box, like a shoebox or something, but the cardboard was sort of damp and you made a nest for it out of a cereal box, and we put a jumper in, do you remember? And it was white, with these little tiny eyes and a pink little mouth, and it was the best present ever? What happened to it, because we weren't allowed pets, were we? It said – something in the lease or something? But he'd just found it in a pile of bin bags on the street, and he'd brought it home?

[Six-second pause]

Q. Do you – I mean you remember that?

J. [Incoherent]

Q. Pardon? I didn't—

J. I said he sat up all the night long feeding it drops of milk from a, a . . . [Wheezing]

Q. Take it easy.

J. A, a, a – a thing. A what-do-you-call-it, a . . .

Q. Syringe?

J. No no no, a . . .

Q. A . . .

J. Pipette. He sat up all night long . . .

Q. Did he? Dad? Are you sure, Mum?

J. [Coughing]

Q. Sorry. I said five minutes, didn't I? I just . . .

[Ten-second pause]

Q. Well – OK, Mum, here's a thing, OK, here's a plan, an idea. I'm going to have to leave you now but if anything occurs to you you can record it, it's easy to do you just press this here, and the light comes on like it is now, and to finish you just – like this . . .

[Recording ends.]

Author's note

In creating the (fictional) documentary on Chernobyl that Lara watches at the start of the narrative I drew heavily on issue 172 of *The Paris Review*, published Winter 2004, which contains Svetlana Alexievich's lucid, precise and devastating compilation of survivors' accounts. I read many articles, accounts and eyewitness testimonies of the disaster as I was researching and creating my 'documentary', but it was Alexievich's interviews that I kept coming back to; in particular the story of Lyudmilla Ignatenko, wife of the deceased fireman Vasily Ignatenko, on whom I based my character of Nastasya. If it had been possible, I would have credited Alexievich's work within the narrative; however, the story demanded that Lara watch a documentary, not read an issue of a literary periodical – and so I would like to take this opportunity to credit it here.

Acknowledgements

The writing of this book was made easier than it might have been by the support of the Arts Council of Northern Ireland. I would like to thank all at ACNI, and in particular Damian Smyth, for their wonderful generosity.

My most grateful thanks are also due to the estates of Sylvia Plath and, most of all, Louis MacNeice, who granted me permission to use words and images that seemed woven so deeply into the fabric of my story I couldn't have reimagined them.

I am extremely fortunate to have worked from an early stage of this book with Angus Cargill, whose thoughts and insights I value most highly. Angus, thank you.

Thank you to Peter Straus, who remains a fearless advocate.

Thank you to Anne Owen and to Merlin Cox, to Becky Pearson and to David Sanger, and to everyone else at Faber who helped with the editing, production and promotion of this book.

Thank you to Paul for the surname, and to Ali for the legal advice, and to Robert for 1970s London. Thank you to Kim for the medical facts and the world of agency carers, and thank you to Donald for the story of a lover in New York. Thank you to Clive for the conversations about poetry and art. Thank you to each and all of my students of the past few years, from whom I've learned so much.

Thank you to Leo and thank you to Rowan, for reading, and rereading, my earliest drafts.

Thank you, Tom, for learning when I needed a safety net and when I just needed to be gone.

And thank you, finally, to Mum and to Dad, to whom this book is dedicated, for more than I can begin to articulate.